THE WILD ONE

THE WILD ONE
ISABEL-CLARA SIMÓ

Translated from Catalan by
Maruxa Relaño and Martha Tennent

3TimesRebel

First published by 3TimesRebel Press in 2025, our fourth year of existence.

Title: *The Wild One* by Isabel-Clara Simó

Original title: *La salvatge*
La salvatge © Isabel-Clara Simó, 1994
By agreement with Pontas Literary & Film Agency.

Translation from Catalan: © Maruxa Relaño and Martha Tennent

Design and layout: Enric Jardí

Cover photography: © Esperanza Manzanera Ferrándiz

Editing and proof reading: Bibiana Mas

Maria-Mercè Marçal's poem *Deriva*:
© heiresses of Maria-Mercè Marçal

Translation of Maria-Mercè Marçal's poem *Deriva*:
© Dr Sam Abrams

The translation of this book is supported
by Institut Ramon Llull.

LLLL institut
ramon llull

Printed and bound by CMP Digital Print Solutions,
Poole, Dorset, England
Paperback ISBN: 978-1-7394528-7-2
eBook ISBN: 978-1-7394528-8-9 / 978-1-7394528-9-6

www.3timesrebel.com

(Estate of) Isabel-Clara Simó, Maruxa Relaño, and Martha Tennent, have asserted their moral rights to be identified respectively as the Author and the Translators of this work.

All rights reserved. Reprinting, online posting or adaptation of the whole or any part of this work without the prior written permission of the Publisher is prohibited except for short quotations as allowed by law in fair use in such as a review.

A CIP catalogue record for this book is available from the British Library.

INDEX

FIRST PART: BLUE

Chapter I – God

1   15

2   23

3. The First Step: Ruler (a)   29

SECOND PART: RED

Chapter II – Jachin

4. The First Step: Ruler (b)   43
5. The Second Step: Gavel (a)   53
6. The Second Step: Gavel (b)   63

Chapter III – Boaz

7. The Third Step: Chisel (A)   71
8. The Third Step: Chisel (B)   79
9. The Fourth Step: Quadrant (a)   87

Chapter IV – Visit
10. The Fourth Step: Quadrant (b)   95
11. The Fifth Step: Level (a)   103
12. The Fifth Step: Level (b)   109

Chapter V – Interiora
13. The Sixth Step: Plumb Line (a)   117
14. The Sixth Step: Plumb Line (b)   125
15. The Sixth Step: Compass (a)   133

Chapter VI – Terrae
16. The Seventh Step: Compass (a)   141
17. The Seventh Step: Compass (c)   143
18. The Seventh Step: Compass (d)   145

THIRD PART: BLACK

Chapter VII – Rectificando
19. The Seventh Step: Compass (e)   149
20. The Sixth Step: Plumb Line (a)   157
21. The Sixth Step: Plumb Line (b)   167

Chapter VIII – Invenies
22. The Fifth Step: Level (a)   175
23. The Fifth Step: Level (b)   183
24. The Fourth Step: Quadrant (a)   191

Chapter IX – Occultum
25. The Fourth Step: Quadrant (b) 199
26. The Third Step: Chisel (a) 205
27. The Third Step: Chisel (b) 213

Chapter X – Lapidem
28. The Second Step: Gavel (a) 219
29. The Second Step: Gavel (b) 227
30. The First Step: Ruler (a) 233

FOURTH PART: WHITE

Chapter XI – Hiram
31. The First Step: Ruler (b) 243
32 249
33 253

Elegy for *Dolores* Mendoza

PART ONE
BLUE

CHAPTER I - GOD
1

THE GIRL WORE AN ANKLE-LENGTH SKIRT MADE OF COARSE material, rumpled and stained, and a shabby sailor's jacket with no buttons. She held it together with both hands, as if giving herself a hug. The scarf on her head—black, or almost black—was knotted at her nape and came down to her eyebrows. On her feet, trainers that must have played many games or walked many a league. Her pale face was covered with freckles; it was dirty, like the moon reflected in a mud puddle.

A gypsy, no doubt, despite the freckles, the frightened blue eyes with eyelashes so blond they were almost translucent. Yes, a gypsy. And therefore, a trickster, and therefore a beggar. She had no business at the door of a gentleman's home. She would only moan and beg and pester. And make demands. Spying through the peephole, Victòria, the maid, decided against opening the door. Even if her curiosity was piqued by that odd-looking girl, so petite she couldn't possibly pose any danger or cause any harm. That year alone there had been five break-ins in the building. Better not take a chance. What if she had an accomplice—what then?

An accomplice lurking about, ready to pounce as soon as you open the door.

Victòria watched over the home. Gentlemen's homes must be watched over by women like Victòria. They must be guarded, these homes where gentlemen sleep and sigh and yawn, where gentlemen who need tending to get their rest and have their meals and stroll about with their hands at their backs. These homes must be guarded even from little gypsy girls with frightened eyes and cheeks of waxen pallor.

The doorbell rang again. So many inventions and yet you can't muffle the sound of that bell or stop it from ringing; eventually it would wake him up, and then he'd say, Don't you know how to answer the door? The idiotic questions he poses, scolding her in that underhanded way of his and making it seem so innocent. They were a twisted lot, masters, every one of them.

Victòria drew back, for the girl, who was still ringing the doorbell, had put her eye to the peephole. She must have caught a glimpse of the dark shadow of Victòria's pupil, and as she looked without seeing—could you see anything from outside?—the girl began to speak. But either her voice wasn't clear enough or that strange little gypsy at the door spoke a language Victòria didn't understand. What could that hideous creature want at a gentleman's home? What was she after? Then the girl's voice reached Victòria. She wasn't exactly shouting; she sounded like she was out of breath. 'Mister Simon! Mister Simon!' Mister Simon? Victòria put her ear to the wooden door and heard the words loud and clear. *Mister Simon.* She cautiously looked through the peephole. The girl was no longer peering inside but holding up a piece of paper. A letter. An envelope, a dirty envelope that had been folded in four and then flattened out. She held it up to the peephole so that Victòria could read what it said, much like a sign is held up at the races to indicate the number of laps.

Victòria was a large, stout woman with broad hips and a wobbly double chin. Her apron was white as dawn, her black hair was pulled back. Her small eyes were buried in a chaos of wrinkles like the pattern left by a bullet hole in a window. There on the envelope, correctly spelled, was Joaquim Simon, her master's name. Words can work miracles, especially written words. Victòria decided to open the door just a crack, enough to accept the letter and send the messenger away. But as soon as she stretched out her hand to grab the paper, the envelope disappeared behind that grubby, loose-fitting skirt as the girl quickly slipped one foot through the door. Victòria would have to shove her away.

A flood of incomprehensible words exploded in Victòria's ears, and though the girl was trying to make herself understood, the words she uttered were all foreign, urgent and incoherent.

'Give me that letter and go away,' Victòria said.

The girl stopped talking; she looked at Victòria and shook her head, as if she could not understand the words but could nevertheless guess their meaning. No longer seen through the encumbrance of the peephole, the girl's eyes shone with fear and desperation. Victòria felt a twinge of pity. They stared at each other for a moment, one set of eyes mistrustful, the other frightened, bright, hard like a frozen lake.

The girl found the words: '*Me see*. Mister Simon.'

Victòria nodded, and the girl seemed to calm down. She removed her arm from behind her back and held up the letter, shaking it like a pigeon that had been grasped by the legs so that it danced about and flapped its wings. The scarf slipped down her nose, and with her left hand she yanked it off her head. It was almost black, the scarf, and it nestled on her shoulders, exposing her ginger hair. There were no redheaded gypsies, no gypsy girls with pale complexions, freckles, and blond eyelashes. A gypsy who wanted to break into a home to steal would never come bearing an envelope with the owner's name. No gypsy uttered foreign words, dark words that conjured up other countries. She must be a foreign gypsy; apparently, they were scattered all over the world. Like rats.

Victòria grabbed the letter in mid-air, gave the girl a gentle shove, and shut the door. 'Wait here,' was all she said. Her tone was stern, and she realized the red-haired girl understood, it seemed to her that she even gave a nod. Letter in hand, and with the half-smile of someone who is doing something bold, Victòria advanced towards the bedroom. 'If he's put out with me for spoiling his nap, he can stuff it,' she grumbled as she went, 'and then he can just stuff it some more. It's his name written here, isn't it? So, if he doesn't like it, to hell with him.'

Words can work miracles, especially written words. The gentleman did not protest at all; being woken up by Victòria meant that one needed to be woken. And besides, why would one sleep if not to be woken? Still in bed, he propped himself up on one elbow, slipped on the glasses that were resting on the bedside table, and glanced at Victòria, who was standing with her hands on her hips, as if challenging him. Suddenly he felt like laughing. Victòria's looked angry, on the defensive. That woman got her knickers in a twist over nothing, over a bloody nap, an absolutely trivial routine. She always made a mole out of an anthill. Life was simpler than that!

He opened the letter and read it. Four hurried lines in rather sloppy English, straight to the point. It was signed by Jack Thurber. The name exploded in his brain like fireworks, and he began to laugh. Nervously, then wholeheartedly. His surprise was such that he read the message again, and then once more. Then he stopped laughing and stared at the letter, sensing that Victòria was watching him, her brow furrowed in disapproval, her mouth half open, her cheeks drooping. She looked like a turtle.

He roared with laughter.

Victòria was offended. She had been so worried about disturbing his sleep, and it was all a big joke to him. 'But it can't be! Impossible!' he was saying. He was almost choking as he slapped the bed, tears streaming down his face. Lunatics need to let off steam, Victòria thought. Live and let live, do your part, and get on with your life. As far as she was concerned, he could pray or sing opera if that's what he wanted.

When the hilarity provoked by the letter subsided, he was suddenly quite pressed. 'So where is this girl?' he asked. On the landing. 'On the landing?' He put on his slippers and his red silk robe and drew the curtains. The enfeebled light of dusk shone on his face. A pot with a wall germander stood on the balcony, its stem reaching upward to caress the air, its one lone flower, purple, swaying lazily, like an old woman in a rocking chair. 'Where else would the girl be?' said Victòria.

'In the drawing room, where one receives visitors? In the shoe cupboard? Out here on the balcony with the plants?'

Ah, silly Victòria, so simpleminded and sensible that she didn't even know she had a sense of humour. How wise she could be, and how foolish. How strong and how weak. Much like everybody else. Aren't we all just a bunch of brutes who steal and usurp, kill and maim, suffer and weep and love in an attempt to cheat death?

Joaquim was shocked when he opened the door. The girl was holding her scarf with both hands, as if about to jump rope, her eyes bright with fever, with fear.

Wait here, the woman had told her. Did these words suggest hope, or did they carry some kind of judgement? The gentleman standing there in the red robe must be this Simon character. His hair was mussed, as if he'd been running or sleeping. All at once he burst out laughing. A curious way to greet people. Thurber had said the man from Barcelona would help her, of this she could be certain, as sure as sunset precedes night. That man who was doubled over with laughter, making fun of her, was old like Thurber. He seemed to live in a palace. She thought she could sooner expect night to fall before sunset than for this man to extend a helping hand.

'And what the devil is your name?' he asked.

The girl understood this was a question, but she didn't know what the question was, so she couldn't answer. She said everything she knew how to say:

'Thurber. Jack Thurber. You, Mister Simon.' And after a short, anxious silence: 'You help me?'

It wasn't the sadness and fear she exuded, or her freckles, or her hair, red like the first light of dawn. It was not the filth she was covered in or the comical figure she cut in her shabby clothes. It was that her voice broke when she said the word *help*, and now she was no longer so amusing to look at. A wave of pity swept over Joaquim Simon as the girl uttered that tremulous 'help me,' and even the plump maid felt it. She was standing there not wanting to miss out, for if you do, then you lose control of things, and then it's over, you are done.

'Victòria, take her to the kitchen and get her something to eat,' he said. 'Then we'll talk.'

His tone was serious, and the girl, as if aided by the universal language of hunger, understood immediately, and she followed Victòria as she retreated into her private domain without glancing back.

2

VICTÒRIA GAVE HER A COLD CHICKEN THIGH, SOME CHEESE and warm milk, a bit of pâté and toast. And biscuits. Seated at the kitchen table, the girl gobbled down the food. She didn't notice that Senyor Simon was watching her. Victòria was relieved, serving food was something she could do almost on instinct, and following instructions was always easier than making decisions. The girl ate and drank hurriedly, without stopping, as if those delicacies might be snatched away at any moment. She looked like a child. How old could she be? Fourteen? Fifteen? Sixteen at most. As she ate, the colour returned to her cheeks, and she was no longer as odd-looking and plain as she had seemed at the front door.

'I'll draw her a bath and see if I can find something for her to wear.' Victòria thrust her chin at the girl's clothes. 'All of that will have to be burned. She stinks.'

The food was so good, so so good! She didn't even look up until she came to the biscuits and bit into them heartily, though her stomach was now full. A brief tremor coursed through her. Senyor Simon was watching her with the air of a professor dissecting a frog in a lab. A new kind of fear welled up inside her and simmered in her brain, the kind of fear that makes a person feel lost, as if wandering the corridors of a vanished home in a forgotten country. The fear of going hungry was a real one, both familiar and concrete. The cold. The dark. A dog's fangs. A beating. Being hounded by the police. Losing one's way. Those were familiar, everyday ghosts, made to measure, like nails that grow to fit the shape of one's fingers. This fear, however, was entirely new. It soured the milk she had just drunk and made sawdust of her chicken and biscuits. Senyor Simon looked at her sternly, and the fear that he aroused in her was abstract, elusive, imprecise. Invisible as the air, yet all too real.

What price would she be made to pay?

The unsettling question shot out of her brain, it bounced off the artsy kitchen tiles and to the microwave, and from there to the refrigerator, then shot straight from the floor to the ceiling and landed on Joaquim's temples. He felt it as if his own thoughts had transformed into words. The sting of pity made him lower his head.

Her hands folded on her skirt, she fought the urge to weep. She had never let anyone see her cry. Having to cross the Atlantic dressed like a buffoon had not made her eyes well up. She had faced the indignity of being hungry, cold, mistreated, scorned. But at that moment she would have wept, if the thought of it hadn't disgusted her so much.

'Now you will bathe and get some sleep.' Joaquim Simon nodded toward the door through which the woman had left to prepare the bath. 'Victòria will buy you something to wear. We'll talk when you're more settled.' He had spoken in English, and the girl had nodded.

I copulated with nothingness, was not shamed or plagued by anything other than the viscous tedium of evening. I was coping. With a sense of trepidation, I opened the door and saw you, Dolores. Then I smiled.

She slept for twelve hours. When she awoke, she couldn't remember where she was. It was five in the morning, and the silence and lack of light blunted her perception. Still naked, she sat up in bed and stared into the dark. The diffuse light of a streetlamp filtered through the lowered blinds. She watched the darkness diminish, her brow furrowed, and felt neither fear nor anguish. It was nice and warm there, it felt good. She was hungry, a good kind of hungry. Slowly, her memory began to recreate her situation, and she remembered that ridiculous fat woman and the man in the red robe. Ah, old Thurber was right!

There was a lamp on the bedside table, and she quickly found the switch. An orb of yellow light revealed a bedroom that belonged in a luxury hotel. Some clothes were laid out on a chair. Braving the cold, she jumped out of bed and looked at the things Victòria had bought for her. A pair of jeans that, lo and behold, were a perfect fit. A shirt that was too big and a jumper that was too tight. Knickers, six pairs of them, and two brassieres, which she had never worn before and immediately tried on. She put on socks and a pair of shoes that were a little loose on her. Everything smelled new, as did her own body after bathing in a round tub so magnificent it was almost sinful.

She tiptoed out to explore. She needed to eat something. Wasn't she a guest there? It wouldn't be stealing. And Thurber's letter had served its purpose; they wouldn't mind if she helped herself to a bit of food. She opened a door and was startled to find a bedroom, probably where that big woman slept. Further along was a living room with a long table, several sofas, a computer, and countless shelves of books. Also, an armchair with buttons; she sat in it and pressed them all, first sitting up, then reclining, then raising the footrest under her legs. It was such fun, almost as much as the horses on a merry-go-round. She felt like laughing, but she knew that at night a house kept the tempo of its sleepers, it held their scent, and her laughter would have resounded like a firecracker.

The third door she tried was the kitchen. It was bathed in an opaque, bluish glow, and the refrigerator shone like the face of the moon. She switched on the light and began to fix herself a bite to eat. Instead of turning on the gas cooker, the button she pressed started an exhaust fan that was hidden in the hood above the stove; instead of milk, wine came out of the carton; instead of butter, that thing was cheese ... but she was hungry, and in the end she managed well enough. It was the best possible breakfast, all by herself, with no one watching her. When she was satisfied, she inspected the living room and the dining area. She took a bottle of whisky from a lighted cabinet and a menthol cigarette from an embossed leather case. She went back to the kitchen to smoke and drink, her feet propped on the table, the chair tilted back, smiling as the light of dawn slowly masked the electric glow of the room. Her mind was empty, she felt pleasantly faint-headed and tipsy.

Victòria found her asleep with her arms on the table cradling her head, still smiling, and reeking of whisky. She would have gladly whacked her with her broom, but seeing how nice she looked in the clothes she had bought for her the previous afternoon while she was taking a bath, and how young and fragile she seemed, a feeling of tenderness came over her. She chased it away by shaking the girl firmly by the arm, and the girl, opening her sleep-clouded eyes, smiled at Victòria as if she was a familiar part of her daily landscape. 'Gracias,' she said in Spanish, and she pinched her sweater to indicate she was referring to her new clothes.

The rest of the conversation was like a game of nonsense, with Victòria shouting as if the girl was deaf—'Whisky, no! Malo!'—and theatrically wagging her finger in front of the girl's nose. It was plain this was not an insult but a clumsy attempt to communicate. And they managed to make themselves understood with their shouting and gesturing, and the sprinkling of Spanish words that the girl remembered. They even laughed when Victòria served up a hearty breakfast and the girl held up two fingers, then rubbed her stomach and puffed out her cheeks. Having breakfast twice was a wonderful thing, and the girl clearly felt good about her double serving, for she started to help Victòria without being asked. Together they cleaned the kitchen, leaving it spick and span and lemon scented; they watered the plants, turned on the heat, and started the washing machine, Victòria shouting her instructions and the girl nodding solemnly.

At ten o'clock, Victòria placed a footed tray on the kitchen table and began to prepare the master's breakfast. When it was ready, she told the girl to follow her, both with gestures and words: 'Sí, sí, come along. We'll take this in and wake him up. He'll be happy to see you looking like a new person in those clothes. It's like night and day, my dear, night and day.' Victòria carried the tray, and the girl slouched behind her, looking a bit like a mouse peeping out of its hole.

The bedroom smelled of sleep, the silky bedspread was as smooth as a baby's bottom. Joaquim was in good spirits and told her that she looked like a princess dressed by a witch. Victòria didn't know any English and couldn't understand what the two of them were laughing about; she seemed almost jealous.

Joaquim asked her to wait in the living room; he'd get dressed and see her there, he wanted to hear the whole story. 'You're Jack Thurber's daughter, right?' 'Nooo.' 'Really?' Suddenly he looked worried, older."You'll tell me about it later.' And he dismissed her with a wave.

Can anyone give an account of their whole life without getting all tangled up? Where does one start? Well, Senyor, I was born ... the thing is, Jack Thurber is a close friend of mine ... well, no, of my father's, actually ... I'm on the run, my life was in danger ... I got a fake passport from Thurber ...

It was no good. That man would never take her in or anything of the sort, at most he'd put her to work with fat Victòria and make a maid of her. He probably didn't owe that old louse Thurber any great favour that had to be repaid.

The door opened. Joaquim Simon entered and with a sigh he plopped himself in the armchair that could be raised or lowered, folded in or extended. His staring eyes sent an unpleasant shudder through the girl, the kind you feel when you are about to sit an exam. And she found herself without a voice.

3
THE FIRST STEP: RULER (A)

'I WAS IN A REAL BIND, YOU SEE, AND MISTER THURBER HELPED me out.'

That bastard Thurber, may he burn in hell for all time.

'He is ... *was* my father's friend. And when everything happened, I went to him for help, and he said to me, here, Dorothy—my name is Dorothy, that's my real name—take this passport, this money, these clothes.'

Foul-smelling old things from that heap of rags soaked with cat urine—revolting!

'And here's this letter, he said to me. Get yourself to Phoenix and onto a plane, and head to Barcelona. That's in Spain. They speak Spanish and Catalan there. You know some Spanish, don't you? Nearly everyone speaks it there. Give the letter to Joaquim Simon, an old friend; he'll lend you a hand. So, I ran out and just managed to make the night bus; the stop is at the far end of town, more than a mile away. And then I waited at the airport for three hours, but at least the passport didn't raise any eyebrows. Thurber told me: Dorothy, wear a scarf on your head, no one will ever believe you're

Hispanic, not with that hair. The passport had belonged to a girl who was a bit older than me. Thurber took my picture in the back room and pressed the tips of my fingers on an inkpad to get my fingerprints, and you couldn't tell at all. Nobody questioned it.'

Joaquim Simon took the passport from his desk and studied the photograph. It was issued in the name of one Dolores Mendoza, nineteen years old, born in Lucena, Spain, daughter of Manuel and Rigoberta Mendoza. That passport, along with a handkerchief full of snot, a tin ring of the kind that comes in a cereal box, and a twenty-five-cent coin, was all that Victòria had found in the girl's skirt pockets.

'Thurber told me not to let anyone know that my name is Dorothy, not Dolores. Only you.'

What an odd name, Dolores. Meaning pains, *plural! The kind of name that fills one's mouth with suffering. I couldn't let Thurber know that my Spanish was not ... well, it was certainly true that there were plenty of Latinos around, quite a few of them at my school, but my neighbourhood was all white. Except for Joe, he was Black. What'll they do without me? They'll think I've been murdered or chased out of town or carried off by the night fog.*

'What kind of relationship did your father and Jack have?' Joaquim Simon asked.

'I'm not sure.' she shrugged. 'They are .... they were friends, I guess, but they didn't see much of each other.'

'Did they ever mention me?'

'No.'

I had never heard of Barcelona either. I didn't even know it existed and couldn't find it on the map. Barcelona was never discussed at school, or if it was, I can't remember. All the way across the ocean! No one who goes there ever returns, they become obsessed with Europe and get stuck there like gnats in the mud. When my father took me to Phoenix a long time ago, I saw an advert for a trip to Venice in a shop window, a holiday package. People from Phoenix do go to Europe to see the sights, but back home in Flagstown ...

'Did Jack tell you why he trusted me, why he was so sure I'd help?'

'No. And besides, there was no time.'

What was I to do? What, exactly? What can you do when your father is being murdered, those two scowling men with vacant eyes strangling him, and your father is going red like he's about to burst, and one of the men turns around and sees you standing barefoot in the doorway, in your nightgown. Grab her, get her, the taller man shouts, and the shorter one bounds toward you, and you run into the street where everything is dark, looking like a ghost in your white nightgown. To Bill's house? No, they won't answer the door. What about the big house, maybe Emmy can hide me? But by the time they hear me knocking and wake up ... Thurber? Thurber! That good-for-nothing who lowers his head when he sees me and doesn't dare look at me, as if he's ashamed or something. Thurber. I didn't know why, but I knew that only he could help me, there was no one else. He was a lowlife, but he owed me big time.

'Did you see them do it—kill him?'

'Pretty much. I ran away as fast as I could and headed to Thurber's house, still in my nightgown. I knocked on the back door, I knew he slept behind his shop. It's just a shack, you know. We used to collect iron scraps from the town dump and take them to him, and he'd pay us for it. The shop entrance is at the front, there's a metal shutter, and inside it's stacked high with stuff, and it stinks. I think there are rats too. I'm not afraid of rats, there are lots of them in the neighbourhood. We, me and my friends I mean, we know how to kill them off, we aren't a bit afraid.'

We start by making lots of noise, pounding the beams with long sticks and screaming like hell. Some of us stand in a semicircle holding sticks with metal spikes. Sooner or later the rats come out, squealing and scurrying about in every which direction. It's easy enough if you're not afraid. I taught Thomas how to hunt them when he moved to the neighbourhood. At first, he was scared, so the rats made straight for him as if possessed. I think they can smell fear. He used to lend me his dog whenever I asked, and I taught him to hunt rats. And not to give in to fear so they wouldn't smell it and attack.

'I knew Thurber was my father's friend, though I never saw them together, but they must have been close. So I knocked at the back of his shop without making too much noise. The door looked rusty and broken, but I knew it worked, and that the old man slept in there. He opened it and gave me a petrified look, not because he knew what had happened, but because he'd been sound asleep. I was probably the last person in the world he expected to come knocking on his door at midnight.'

After that thing happened, I always took the longer route so I wouldn't have to walk past the store. It was the only thing in the world that really scared me. That and my teeth falling out, like poor Jeremiah, who looked like an old geezer with his empty gums. When Father found out, he stormed over to Thurber's to have it out with him. He'll kill him, I told myself. He'll kill him! And the thought of my father beating that filthy beast to a pulp filled me with joy. But when Father returned—in the end he really wasn't such a bad father—he looked at me as if he was ashamed, and said, 'Don't go bothering Mister Thurber again. And keep away from his shop.' He downed a big jigger of gin, something he reserved for special occasions, and gave me a sideways glance. And he added: 'Don't worry, he won't touch you again.' That was the day I became an adult. I never again believed anything my father said, and I no longer wanted to hear his stories about his time in the Marines or about the look on my mother's face the day she left, or about how Uncle Ted used to walk on his hands when he was in the circus. I no longer believed him because I had suddenly grown up, and now I saw him for what he was: a sad, shrivelled-up old man who could only brag when he was down at Hoolys, the local bar, because everyone had tired of him a long time ago. But when those two men came for him, with their long faces and vacant eyes, and I ran as fast as I could, it occurred to me that only Thurber could help. If there had been some kind of secret between him and Father, I would use it to my advantage. Besides, he owed me, didn't he? If I'd gone to the police and told them what that disgusting man had done to me ... I was only thirteen when it happened. They would have thrown him in jail, and the other inmates would have let him have it good. I've heard that, in prison, they don't go easy on men who hurt women and girls ... but maybe the police wouldn't have believed me, and my father wouldn't have backed me up. Boy, did Thurber owe me! I was sure he'd hide me until the guys who killed Father were gone. They wouldn't find me there. I'd stay very still, and old Thurber would peep through a crack, both of us crouching in the dark. And when they'd left, he'd say, 'all right, girl, you can leave now.' I was sure he wouldn't lay a finger on me. I don't know why, but I was sure. Just as I was sure that he would hide me until those men got tired of combing the neighbourhood looking for me. They couldn't stay there long, or they might get caught. Instead, Thurber asked lots of questions, grabbing me by the shoulders and shaking me as if I was a bottle of ketchup and he was trying to squeeze out the last bit. Frantic, he was. 'So, you saw it then? Did you see their faces? Did they look like this, like that?' And then: 'You've got to get out of here, girl. They'll hunt you down if you don't do exactly as I say.' At first, I didn't want to; those two men wouldn't dare come back, no matter how afraid they were that I'd be able to describe them. They'd killed a man, hadn't they? And even if it was a total nobody like my father, a man with weak lungs from working down in the copper mines, who had a miserable pension and was always down at Hoolys getting drunk and showing off—he was still a man, no? Killing someone is a crime. But I started getting scared. Thurber said those men weren't working alone, they were part of a bigger organisation, and the skin on my bones wasn't worth any more to them than a rabbit pelt. I had to do as he said. He took my picture and my fingerprints and spent more than half an hour forging a passport. I rummaged through a pile of old clothes, trying to find something to wear. I couldn't go home to get anything. Not even my shoes. Or the box of peppermints that held my savings. And all I could find at Thurber's was a bunch of raggedy old things that reeked of cat urine. How I hate cats! Revolting creatures. Thurber kept saying: 'You have to dye your hair black. Your name is Dolores now. You understand? Do-lo-res. Say it, so you won't forget. I don't think they'll go after you, not all the way to Barcelona. That's a long way from here.' He couldn't find any hair dye among all the piles of junk and filthy clutter, so he told me to colour my hair at the airport. Are you allowed to do that, just go in the bathroom like that and dye your hair with everyone watching?

'And he helped me,' she said. 'He put a scarf on my head and pulled it down, so you couldn't tell I was a redhead.'

'Your father and Jack,' Joaquim Simon said, 'did they get together sometimes? With other people, like in a kind of club or something, once a week maybe?'

'I don't think so. I just recall father coming and going a lot, doing odd jobs, some gardening, a bit of construction work.'

'Flagstown was the name of the town?'

'It's actually a city, it's quite big and really beautiful, but we didn't exactly live in Flagstown, our neighbourhood is Colorado Moon. Everyone calls it Moon. It's on the outskirts. There used to be a foundry there, but that was before I was born. Now all we've got is the dump. There are only two streets, and an esplanade with dry grasses and rotten beams. We don't even have a school or anything, and no bus service. Finney, a Black guy who owns a truck, used to give me a ride to school, but I had to walk home, and I got tired of that. Once you get beyond the scattered beams that are piled higher than a person, you come to a shallow ravine. The bottom is boggy, but we used wooden planks and sheets of zinc and built a kind of gangway to get across to the flats on the other side. The Little Colorado River is right there. It's dangerous to swim in, but we all do when it's hot, and it gets really hot in Moon. You can see Humphreys Peak, always snow-capped 'cause it's so tall.'

She came from a place that was a hole in the ground, that girl. She was a wild thing. And Thurber and her father and the rest of them came from the same pit of losers, where people boozed and quarrelled and beat one another, where truant youngsters hunted rats. Joaquim Simon smiled remembering the good old times with his pal Thurber, living in Los Angeles and feeling on top of the world. He took another look at the fake passport—it was good, that bastard still had skills—and considered the strange, freckled face of this wild child.

'I'll call you Dolores,' he said. 'Always. We'll tell everyone that your name is Dolores and you're an orphan, a relative of mine.'

'Does that mean I can stay?'

Joaquim Simon smoothed out the letter. Just four scribbled lines. *The girl is the daughter of a friend. He's been killed and now they're after her. Please take her in. And don't let anyone know I'm the one who sent her. Remember William Morgan?* And below this, the signature: Jack Thurber.

William Morgan died in New York City in 1926; he met a terrible end, and no one ever found out who murdered him.

Neither he nor Jack had any connection to the man, but to them his name was shorthand for vicious revenge. Morgan, a journalist and a feisty lush, was a divisive figure. He and Jack respected him. Morgan had balls, there was no denying that.

From that brief letter, it was impossible to tell what exactly had happened. On first impression, Joaquim Simon could have sworn that the person in trouble was Jack, and this girl was his daughter ...

'Of course you can stay,' he said.

'As your maid?'

'Maid?' Joaquim Simon looked surprised and laughed again, the same way he had when he first saw her standing at the door.

To get to Barcelona, Dolores had taken three flights; the money from Thurber covered the plane tickets, but just barely. She'd been served a meal on one of the flights, on the other two she'd gotten candy and a Coca-Cola. People eyed her as if she were a feral creature. Was it her fault if the only thing Thurber could provide were some rags that stank of cat pee? It had taken her four long hours to find her way from the airport to Mister Simon's home. She couldn't make herself understood. There were no Hispanics in Colorado Moon, and she had only heard Spanish being spoken at school, but she'd never paid much attention. She told Thurber that she spoke Spanish to make things easier. Sometimes she lied just to avoid having to explain. To conserve energy. No one could understand her in Barcelona, so she was sent from one place to the next; sometimes people turned away without even acknowledging her, as if her mere existence was offensive. You're nothing but a bunch of Hispanics, she told herself.

It was mid-afternoon by the time she found the street. More than a street, it was actually a cul-de-sac ringed by apartment buildings with gardens. To reach the place you had to climb a steep street that wound its way up a hill. Number six was in the middle. There was a waist-high iron gate with spikes, and two long planters flanked the front entrance. The plants had no flowers. Rose bushes don't grow in winter, and their scrawny branches were shrivelled up like an old crone that had been left out in the cold. The door to the building was closed, but there were grilled windows on either side, and the one on the right was ajar. It was easy enough to slip her fingers through and open the door from the inside. The lobby had leather sofas and light fixtures on the walls, and even radiators. There were three floors in the building, as she had already noticed, and on the first floor she found a plaque with the name that was written on her envelope. She was in luck. She was about to ring the doorbell when, all at once, she panicked. She gritted her teeth. Fear can either be swallowed or spat out; her fear was smooth and pliable like well-chewed gum. She swallowed it.

'Maid?' Joaquim Simon repeated. 'No, you'll be my daughter. You can't stay here indefinitely unless you have a residence permit. I'll adopt you. Your name is Dolores, that is what you will tell everyone, and I mean everyone, including Victòria.' He raised a menacing finger. 'You hear me?'

His daughter? The man was off his rocker. Can people just invent a daughter?

'I'll take care of the details,' he said. 'I have a first-rate solicitor. We'll pretend you are an orphaned niece of mine, all alone in the world, and I want to adopt you. There won't be any trouble.'

'What do I have to do?' she said in a thin voice.

'You? Nothing at all, just do as I say, that's it.' As if the thought had just occurred to him, his forehead clear and smooth, he slowly told her: 'Get this through your head, just this one thing. You will follow my rules, and the rules are that I want you pretty, I want you cultured, and I want you strong. And straight as an arrow.'

PART TWO
RED

CHAPTER II – JACHIN

4
THE FIRST STEP: RULER (B)

SHE TOLD THEM SHE WAS FIFTEEN, THOUGH SHE WOULDN'T be until May. And that she got her hair from her mother, who looked like a model but had passed away, poor dear, from lung disease. She diligently answered all the questions the barrister and judge asked. She said she would like to go by her adoptive father's surname rather than Mendoza, and she didn't want her name to be Dolors, in Catalan, but Dolores, for that's what she was used to being called, even if she hated that the name meant *pains*. The more she lied, the better she got at it. Joaquim Simon—Quim—glanced at her with approval, encouraging her.

It was all so exciting, and Dolores swore she would be all those lovely things her new father wanted her to be. School, on the other hand, was out of the question. She refused to go. Joaquim had no other choice but to homeschool her. They got off to a good start, but the demands of teaching soon became a burden, and he grew impatient and hired a sad-looking young fellow with grey eyes and thick glasses. Dolores was thrilled. Her new teacher, Tomeu, was a gullible fool that could easily be led up the garden path, something she would never have done with Quim.

Tomeu reminded Dolores of her friend Thomas when he first moved to Colorado Moon. He had a piercing gaze, but he was reticent, so thin and quiet, as if his words were stuck in his throat and refused to come out. One day the two of them went down to Little Colorado River for a swim and Thomas was too embarrassed to take off his clothes, so they sat together in silence and gazed at the river, at the changing sunset, always a different shade of red. And suddenly Thomas said: 'Father beats me.' All fathers beat their children, what else are fathers for? But no one ever talked about it. What Thomas really meant was *I'm your friend, so I'm confiding in you.* From that moment on, she protected him. She taught him how to hunt rats, and to always look Bill in the eye without lowering his gaze. Bill wasn't such a bad person, but he was very full of himself, and he enjoyed intimidating others. Thomas found a cave, and she told the others about the discovery. That's how Thomas became part of the gang, so much so that when he showed up one day with a split lip no one even mentioned it. Everyone should deal with their own problems. Joe suggested they head to the gas station to see about getting their hands on some cash. Hugh, the manager, kept the tip jar by the window, and when he was distracted, you could reach in and grab a few coins; the man never counted them anyway. When Thomas said, 'I'm out,' no one laughed or challenged him. That meant he was one of them.

It wasn't that Tomeu looked anything like Thomas, but they were both thin and sad. And neither of them smiled. Quim monitored their progress and was never satisfied. She wasn't straight as an arrow like he wanted her to be, and that embarrassed her.

She didn't have any friends in the building. There were only three apartments, one on each floor. A notary and his wife, both nasty and stuck-up, lived above them, and on the top floor there was a family with two children, a stupid son who was about her own age and a younger daughter, the kind of young people who have no curiosity and never make any friends. They blasted music when their parents were out and laughed loudly on the stairs, they littered the foyer with sunflower seed shells and wiped their feet on other people's doormats. Victòria couldn't stand them, and if Quim hadn't stopped her, she would have often headed upstairs to give them a piece of her mind. 'We don't choose our family or neighbours, only our friends,' he would say. 'We must resign ourselves to our country, our blood, and our neighbours.' He would give Dolores a faint smile that might have meant that family was trouble even when it was chosen, or maybe that she was an exception to the rule. But the worst thing was the cat that lived upstairs with that weird family. Dolores hated it even more than most cats, and it always seemed to be waiting for her on the stairs. Couldn't they keep their door shut? Couldn't they be like normal people and have a dog? Apparently not. The mother of those two brats, who had feline features herself, had not wanted a dog, she said they were too much trouble. They had given that stupid cat the ridiculous name of Foof. And whenever Dolores went out, there it was, peering at her. Horrid creature! She would kick it, but instead of keeping its distance, Foof lingered on the stairs as if waiting for her, no doubt plotting revenge.

The best place in the apartment was the kitchen, with Victòria, who told her everything she needed to know. Now that she could understand what she was saying, Dolores learned more about Joaquim from her than she could have gleaned through mere observation. Victòria was not above criticizing her master, though with a certain warmth. 'Make sure you wash your hair, don't make me cross,' she'd say. 'Senyor wants it nice and shiny. And you must brush it every night; it's all you've got, your hair, so don't be daft, use it to your advantage!' Dolores liked Victòria's no-nonsense approach to life, it was something she could understand. And when Victòria scolded her, which was often, she was like a bad-mouthed farmer cursing at her own field and calling it names, only to then turn around and water, plough and fertilize the land, as if those two sentiments, love and hate, were in harmony.

One day Joaquim sent them to the beauty salon. Inside, there were sweet smells and music in the air, and made-up girls who spoke in soft voices, as if they had marvellous secrets to tell. The windows were blacked out. 'This girl's freckles,' Victòria said to them, 'they need to go.' She explained that Senyor, that is, her father, did not like them.' A girl with lavender eye shadow and long nails laughed and said they couldn't be removed, not even cosmetic surgery would do the trick. But they had something that would lighten them. 'She won't be able to sunbathe. If she goes in the sun her freckles will come out again, same as before.' She said they were charming and went well with her red hair. 'Look at Katherine Hepburn, such a big success in Hollywood, the toughest place to crack, with a redhead's complexion and her hair up in a bun. What counts is making the most of what you've got.'

Victòria was in a foul mood when they got home. She told Joaquim that everyone had their own looks and kind of face, and it was wrong to meddle with it. But she had bought two jars of face cream that promised to lighten Dolores's freckles. Quim frowned and scrutinized the girl, and declared that perhaps her freckles weren't classy, but they had their charm. And besides, refined people were a dime a dozen. He told Dolores to apply the cream every night.

On another occasion, he got very cross and shouted at her about her table manners. Dolores was stunned. Imagine telling her she didn't know how to eat, when she'd been doing it all her life! Joaquim showed her how to use the cutlery, the napkins and glasses, what could be eaten with one's fingers and what could not. But then he saw her biting her nails and he stormed out, slamming the door behind him.

In the kitchen, however, everything was clear and easy to understand.

'He says I don't know how to read properly, Victòria. Or eat. He didn't tell me I don't know how to sleep because he doesn't see me doing that. If he did, I'm sure he'd tell me I was doing it wrong.'

'Just go along with what he says,' Victòria told her. 'Don't you see he's a bit barmy? And don't talk back.'

'I never talk back. It's so hard being a daughter. The way he stares at me, it gives me the creeps!'

'Here's an idea. Whenever he gets upset with you, just stand in the sunlight and let your hair shine. He loves your hair. Take advantage of it, girl, use what you've got.'

As if he had overheard the conversation, Joaquim only told her off at night or when the curtains were drawn. Dolores would toss her hair to see if that would placate him, but it only made him angrier. 'Why are you jerking your head like that?' he'd say. 'Is behaving like a wild thing all you know how to do?'

Victòria told Dolores that Joaquim did not have to lift a finger to make money. People would phone him up looking for investors and offering business opportunities. If he trusted them, Quim would study their proposal and make some phone calls or invite Jon Carnisser, his solicitor, to dinner, and they would sit talking until dawn. He would weigh all the pros and cons before making a decision. And because he was clever, he almost always got it right, and then more money would flow in. If he ever failed, he would mope around for a while. 'This money thing is like the weather,' he would tell Victòria. 'Sometimes it rains and sometimes it doesn't. But it's only money.'

Victoria said that before she arrived, Quim had hosted evening parties at the apartment for a group of friends who liked to drink and have a good time. But now he didn't want any visitors. 'He's ashamed of you,' Victòria said. 'As soon as he's got you trained to his liking, they'll be back. Senyor must have the best of everything. And what is the best of everything for? Not to enjoy it, no. It's so his friends will ooh and aah over it. Once he's sure they'll adore you, they'll all be back. And you'll smile and know what to do.'

Dolores applied herself, she studied hard and did what she was told, but she found herself growing impatient. It all seemed so senseless and boring. But then she would look at her clothes, at the neat row of shoes, all brand new, and the underwear drawer brimming with lovely things, and she would tell herself to stop being a fool and to enjoy life now that it was all smooth sailing. It would have been easier if she had a friend to talk to, but there was only Victòria, and that big grumbling woman was not enough.

One morning, she met the boy from the bakery. Ramon was only fourteen, and on weekdays he delivered bread and croissants to the family on the third floor. Dolores ran into him on her way in from the garden and they chatted for more than half an hour. They soon became friends. Ramon saved the pastries that came out misshapen for her. Dolores begged Victòria to let her buy the bread. Ramon promised to bring his dog along one day, because she had mentioned how much she liked them, but it would have to be after closing time; his boss wouldn't allow dogs in the bakery. Dolores made him a lucky charm that was a nicely splayed spider held between two glass buttons. Ramon said it made a magnificent amulet. Would it help with tooth cavities?

One Sunday, with the first heat of summer, Dolores hurriedly got ready to sneak out of the apartment to play football with Ramon. *I'll teach you English football and you teach me American football. Deal?* There on the landing was that nasty Foof, baring its teeth in spiteful silence, glaring at her. She ignored it and raced down the stairs, but the animal followed her, panting like an old hag running to catch a bus. Dolores was almost to the gate when the cat pounced on her and scratched her cheek.

She exploded with pent-up rage. 'I'll show you who I am, you beast!' She grabbed the cat by the scruff of its neck, swung it around and, wheee, flung it toward the wall. If it died, so be it; no one would point a finger at her. With a screeching yowl, the animal sailed through the air and landed atop the gate, its belly impaled on a spike. It lay there like a cotton rag draped on the gate. The iron bar oozed blood. For a moment, the cat's glassy eyes were open, then its head drooped. It looked like a stuffed animal that had been caught on the metal spike.

Dolores was filled with disgust. If the cat had hit the wall, she could have killed it off with two more kicks and tossed it into the street, and people would have thought it had been run over by a car. The thought of pulling the soft black body off the spike made her want to vomit, so she headed up to the apartment to look for Victòria. She found her kneeling on the big rug, removing stains with a pungent liquid, her face red, her gartered white thighs, which were threaded with blue veins, showing. 'You are a nasty piece of work,' Victòria said when she heard what had happened. She went to the kitchen to fetch a binbag and a couple of rags and grabbed a large shovel from the tool cupboard. 'Come and make yourself useful,' she said.

Without a word, Victòria lifted the cat off the spike; she looked pale as she stuffed the animal's body into the binbag. Then she took it round the back to the small garden. The earth beneath the lemon tree that grew by the bougainvillea was soft, like the sand on a beach. Dolores started digging. After they buried the cat, Victòria wiped the bars on the gate, spitting on the spots where the blood had congealed. Then she went back upstairs. She threw the bloodied rags in the rubbish bin and gave Dolores a look the girl had never seen before, her eyes lost in a sea of wrinkles. Then she slapped her.

That night after dinner, Joaquim called Dolores to his study. He scolded her with sadness, but there was no yelling. He seemed much older, there were bags under his eyes, his cheeks were sunken. And he looked at her as if she inhabited that place at the centre of his world and soul where all disappointments lie.

Dolores had never felt such an urge to cry; she was barely able to hold back until she was in her room with the door shut. She sat in front of the vanity mirror and unburdened herself of the pain caused by Joaquim's disappointment. She wept like a punctured water balloon, a deflating wineskin losing the spirit that had made it beautiful. The tears made the scratch on her cheek burn, and her weeping image in the mirror filled her with disgust at being weak, ugly, a brute. Snip, snip, snip. With a few clips of the large scissors, Dolores cut off her hair. The long red strands that fell on the dressing table looked like dead copperheads.

Joaquim did not speak to her for two weeks. But he did not tell the upstairs neighbours what had happened to the cat.

5
THE SECOND STEP: GAVEL (A)

IN A YEAR, HAIR GROWS OUT. IN A YEAR, A YOUNG GIRL'S breasts become high and fragrant, full and firm. *Pale and rede and blonde/ was the fair Dolores ...* as was Blanquerna, the hero in the medieval novel. Ramon, the bread boy, was no longer good enough for her, and Tomeu, the sad teacher, resigned his post, too unsettled by Dolores's charms.

Aim to become not ignorant, but wise, not fanatical, but tolerant, not ambitious, but generous. That's what Joaquim had told her. Dolores applied herself, and when she found that she lacked know-how, she just gave a lopsided smile and coyly lowered those blond eyelashes of hers, and then her cheeks dimpled and her teeth gleamed white and she looked like such a sweet young girl. She's not so wild after all, Victòria would think. But Joaquim's heart was cold, his manner toward Dolores was gruff, and when she put on the charm act, he simply measured the length of her hair. He did this on the first day of the month, commenting on the growth, whether it was one or two centimetres longer. Then he would angrily send her away.

In the bathroom, while shaving, Joaquim considered his wizened face and stroked his cheeks with dark melancholy. He was not scared of death itself, but of dying. He recalled the good times in America, when he and Jack had been as poor as church mice, and thought about Joseph what's-his-name, the Jew, and the society they founded with the backing of a certain Jean-Paul Nicolas who said he was a count. After Joaquim made his money and returned home, he continued to mingle with members of the society, which had chapters all over the world. But he had grown old and disenchanted, he no longer believed in anything now, and he never attended those secret meetings.

Joaquin finished getting ready. Jon Carnisser was about to arrive, and he wanted it to be a splendid occasion. It would be the first time Dolores would be allowed to take part in a social gathering, and Joaquim hoped to introduce her with the cheery boastfulness with which one might offer a spring pear plucked from a tree that has been carefully cultivated. His stomach was churning.

'This girl is an agent of destruction,' he told his friend. 'They raised her like a stray dog, but I will tame her. I'm a strict father, believe me, but I haven't seen much progress yet.'

For an entire year, I have scarcely allowed her out of the apartment, and then only around the neighbourhood, and only with Victòria. She's clever, a quick study, but she's still a wild filly who will only accept her bridle in exchange for gifts.

Reclining in his chair, Jon Carnisser gazed at Joaquim through his glass of Armagnac and smiled. 'You would like for her to be a piece of ivory that you could carve.'

'She's still a girl,' Joaquim said. 'But I must admit I rather like the idea of finding out whether I've got what it takes to mould a child to my liking. Don't be too warm toward her over dinner. Think of it as an exam she must pass.'

In the kitchen, Dolores and Victòria were making sweet potato tarts, candied chestnuts, and marzipan *panellets*.

'He wants me to be perfect and never make a mistake,' Dolores said.

'The only thing he wants is for your hair to be as long as it was at the beginning,' Victòria said. 'And for you to behave. He's very stubborn, you know, and he's got it into his head to make a proper lady out of you. There's no way out of this now.'

'I wonder if he'll ever forgive me for the hair.'

'Forgive you? He doesn't know the meaning of the word!'

It was a warm November, a smell of forest hung in the air. In the garden in front of the building, the bright green leaves of the acacia drooped and trembled. Three distinct colours tinged the sky, and a long, snake-like cloud propped up the sun, preventing it from slipping behind the Collserola mountain range. A flock of starlings practiced the perfect geometry of communal flight.

'It's the first time he's having someone over.' Victòria passed Dolores a jar of pine nuts to coat the round panellets. 'That's a good sign.'

'Yes, but it's only this one person, and he's a good friend. Quim doesn't trust me yet; he just doesn't.'

'Don't you dare eat that, you cheeky girl!' Victòria scolded her. 'Now, listen up. Don't talk with your mouth full, don't interrupt when they're speaking or let the conversation peter out, don't argue, don't rest your elbows on the table, and remember to use your napkin to wipe your mouth after drinking ... '

'Too much!' Dolores protested. 'Back where I grew up, there was this Black man named Finney who owned a lorry; he taught me how to drive. I thought I couldn't possibly remember to do so many things at the same time, but then ... You know what I'd really like, Victòria? To go to the beach!'

'Right. And catch pneumonia.'

'But it's so warm out!'

'At first, my curiosity was piqued,' Joaquim was saying. 'Then I took it as a challenge. I'll go about it in such a way it can't possibly be improved upon. That's what I told myself. Education is a question of method. People aren't all that different from machines; we just have more buttons that can be pressed, and we have to learn what they are for.'

'You are incorrigible, Joaquim!' said Jon Carnisser. 'And this girl, does she really see you as some kind of monster?'

'I hope so, and it helps that Victòria does too. They're preparing dinner together. Dolores isn't supposed to help, she does it behind my back.'

'Don't you get bored, Joaquim, living like a hermit in here, supervising things and making increasingly lofty demands?'

'The only thing that truly bores me is human stupidity, and there's plenty of that to go around. Besides, I'm getting old.' Joaquim paused, as if taking a moment to savour his brandy. 'Do I seem terribly old to you? I mean, am I all washed up?'

Victòria was sitting in a chair, her hands resting on her lap, her face flushed. It was dark outside. Dolores switched on the light, but Victòria asked her to turn it off; her eyes were bothering her. She was waiting for the oven timer to ring. Her tone was melancholy: 'He was seventeen years old, very tall, with curly hair like his father. He had an easy laugh. When I got the news, he was already dead; he crashed his motorcycle into a lorry and hit the radiator.'

His skull was smashed like a melon that had been cracked open with a stone. It didn't look like him at all. The doctor kept saying he was already dead when they brought him in, and it wasn't his fault. Seventeen years old, lying there with his face smashed, his eyes cloudy like fisheyes. I didn't want to cry. I felt ill. My belly ached as if it had been emptied out and there was only a hole there, no bowels, no spleen, no bladder, no ovaries, no womb. Just an empty hole. How it throbbed! I didn't want to live. Life weighed so heavily on me. But then I was able to feel my belly again, as if my insides were back in their rightful place, and I was suddenly ravenous. I was ashamed to give in to hunger. I ate, but then I felt nauseous, and when I didn't eat I had the most terrible pangs. The doctor prescribed something to help me sleep, but I took it all day long, and that's how it was for ten straight days. I ate and vomited, took pills, and lay in bed at night with my eyes open, unable to sleep. During the day, I slept in a chair. I couldn't think about Octavi, or I would not have been able to carry on. So I thought about lace or embroidery work or about making coca de llardons, *things that entail effort. And I remembered when I used to knead bread or make soap at home. I would think about the cold until I shivered and about the heat until I began to sweat. Ten days of this.*

It was getting darker, and past the time they had set for dinner. Victòria had turned her chair away to face the oven; her shoulders drooped like the wings of a bird that is curled up in the cold. Dolores was seated too, attuned to the silence that emanated from the older woman. She had only bitten one of her nails, and she had applied cream every night, so her hands were soft and delicate. She rubbed them together.

'I didn't want to cry,' Victòria said. 'If I started, I might never stop. I tore up all the pictures without looking at them, so I could cope. But that's not possible. Not like that, or any other way.'

The kitchen smelled of warm oven and tears, it smelled of panellets, and it was dark. The women sat in their chairs waiting for the oven timer to ring. In the study, Senyor and his friend chatted away, probably discussing money or women or some other nonsense. There's no understanding men.

The timer went off. Victòria switched on the light, turned off the oven, and removed a smoking tray of panellets. They looked store-bought, though perhaps a little flat, but that was because they were homemade and didn't have any potato in them. These were the real thing, no shortcuts. A wave of nausea swept over Dolores. She was afraid she wouldn't be able to eat any of the delicacies they had made for their guest.

Dolores was not allowed to lay the table or do any housework, but she would slip into the kitchen and help Victòria because Joaquim never set foot in there. And now there was nothing left to do in that room that was redolent of warm oven and tears. The moment had arrived for Dolores to make her way to the study and sit with the men making conversation while Victòria lay the table. Joaquim introduced their guest, Jon Carnisser. The sadness that suddenly overcame Dolores kept her from paying enough attention to make a good impression. She sat listening but said nothing, despondent. The gentleman asked lots of questions, and though she was usually glad to see people and converse, now she was at a loss for words, her mouth dry. Joaquim shot her an angry look. Dolores was failing her first real test. The practical component.

Victòria announced that supper was ready: they could move to the dining room. Then she took a look at the girl, noted Joaquim's mood and the strange expression on the guest's face, and she decided to take Dolores with her, whether her master liked it or not. The ghost of her curly-haired boy was a gut-wrenching memory. She untied her apron right there, in front of the solicitor, whom she knew well. 'The girl and I are off to the cinema,' she announced. 'We'll be back! Enjoy your supper.' A shocked Joaquim watched the two of them go without saying a word. Jon laughed at his friend and gave him a slap on the back.

It was a boring movie. Victòria fell asleep and snored a little. Dolores used the cover of darkness to weep, as if the film were making her sad. She didn't know why she was crying. At home, in the dining room, the two gentlemen ate sweet potato tarts, candied chestnuts, and panellets. They drank muscatel wine. Jon Carnisser didn't have the heart to continue poking fun at Joaquim, so they talked about politics and women, as was their wont. He even managed to get a smile out of Quim.

Joaquim was alone in the living room reading a book when Victòria and Dolores got home. He didn't greet them. Dolores wasn't hungry, so she went to bed without dinner. She pulled the covers around her, remembering the times when her father was in a good mood and used to bring her little treats, mostly candy that he hid in the inside pocket of his sport jacket. She thought about Thomas, about Little Colorado River, about how rich she was now. And how lonely. A ball of fire burned in the pit of her stomach; she felt ill. She kicked off the covers. How nice it would be to have a swim in that river, even though it was November, and it would be freezing. She could almost feel the water cooling her body.

In the middle of the night, Joaquim tiptoed into her room once again. Filled with bitterness, he stood watching her in the abandon of sleep. Dolores didn't know that he also scrutinized her sleep.

A sleeping body. A body that animates the rhythmic panting of unconsciousness. Finally at rest, freed from the head's haughty weight, the neck bends, and strands of hair cling to it with the fragrant perspiration of sleep. A cheek nestles on a hand, the hand on the pillow; the lips part, but only slightly, and a soft flutter of captive pupils troubles the eyelids, seeking the light. Yours is the scent of a sleeping body. At the end of the bed, a foot peeps out. I weep the tears of an enfeebled old man, obstinate, sentimental. The soles of your feet are pink, Dolores, and this moves me.

The following day, during her geography lesson, Dolores apologized for making a bad impression.

'I was out of sorts,' she said.
'And now? Are you feeling better?'
'I'm not sure.'
'Enough of this nonsense!'
'The thing is—'
'What is it, what's wrong?'
'It's just that ... well, I would love to go to the beach.'

Joaquim didn't laugh at this. They finished their first lesson, then maths, then the daily essay. He seemed absent-minded; he didn't once scold her. The following day, they drove up to Blanes and had lunch at a restaurant that was right on the beach. The sea had risen, as if it had been baked with yeast, and the seagulls squawked through the air. The foamy waves were grey, the sky was laden with mud. Just as they were finishing their lunch, it started to rain. As if enlivened by the static in the air, Dolores started laughing and talking. Then she rushed out in the rain. Through the restaurant window, Joaquim watched her running barefoot through the wet sand and opening her mouth to taste the raindrops. He saw that tanned white body, that blazing head of hair in the rain and he was filled with melancholy.

6
THE SECOND STEP: GAVEL (B)

JOAQUIM SIMON TOOK WHATEVER MONEY HE COULD FIND AND left the pieces of the broken radio on the desk in his father's study. He was thirteen years old. Carrying with him a large suitcase full of clothes, he fled just as the night was lifting and the sinister spectre of war was spreading across the world. He couldn't stand his whingeing father and mother and little sister, and he had no wish to be a mathematician or a solicitor, the only options available to him. Above all, he would no longer tolerate his father's embittered, humiliating, degrading brutality. He had taken the radio Quim had been given for Three Kings Day and flung it against the wall. It was Quim's radio, and he loved it.

How he hated the priests at school, and the smart alecks they always set as examples, the nasty droolers and arse-lickers; that's why he cut class, often enough that in the end the headmaster alerted his father. And his father beat him and broke his radio, his one source of pride. None of his friends owned one and they all envied him. The frame was made of solid wood, and he polished it until it shone. It was beautiful.

Running away from home was a bit like skipping school, just for a longer period of time. When he left, he felt nothing but rage. No fear, no remorse, no regrets. Being thirteen doesn't make you a simpleton, it doesn't even mean you're naïve; he was equipped for the journey and had enough money. He never went back.

He would have preferred Venezuela, where all you had to do was hold out your hand and they gave you money, but his ship set sail for the United States of America. He tried to avoid scrutiny; if one of the crew was watching him, he would strike up a conversation with some elderly lady, and everyone assumed he was travelling with his family. He was smartly dressed, well-behaved, and clever. The waves that broke on the ship's bow were like the bell announcing that school was out, they resounded in his heart and made it sing. He did not regret leaving home; he trained his eyes on the heaving surface of the water and whispered: 'Fuck you, fuck you, fuck you all.' Perhaps the curse he spat into the sea ensured that his parents' many attempts to find him were in vain.

On reaching Ellis Island, he underwent a medical and legal inspection. He had to sharpen his wits to get into New York City. He said he was there to see his father, who worked in the city, but he couldn't provide a plausible address, and they didn't believe him. Then he pretended he had been travelling with his mother, and she had thrown herself overboard one night during the crossing and he, shattered as he was, had not dared tell the captain. But there was no record of her name on the passenger list. When they had already decided to send him back, he managed to hide in a trunk that belonged to an Italian student. It was filled with books, which he tossed into the sea. The few airholes he made in the trunk did not prevent him from almost dying of suffocation. By the time he cleared the last hurdle, he was in such a state that he curled up by the entrance to a building, his cheeks drained of colour, and he lay there like an old rag for several hours.

The stringent immigration controls of the 1930s had loosened considerably by the 40s, and it didn't take long for him to realize that New York City was full of illegals like himself. The money soon ran out, and he was forced to take a string of odd jobs. He learned the language in no time, the priests had already taught him some English, though his French was better. When his last dime was gone and he was evicted from a sinister boarding house of the kind where questions are never asked, he realized his moment of reckoning had come. Working as a shoeshine boy, running errands, or opening car doors for customers were not options, the competition was fierce, organized, and often violent. The few times he tried, he had been given a beating, but he had something his competitors lacked: good manners and good clothes. A cheap hotel in Brooklyn hired him as a bellhop, and he was attentive and helpful, so everyone tipped him. The job came with a place to sleep, a room tucked away in the attic. His stroke of luck was being decent at tennis: a guest at the hotel suggested they play together and offered to pay for it. The man took him to a sports club. Joaquim made a few contacts there, but he had to be careful; the club turned a blind eye if a member brought a guest, but if they got wind that he was trying to make a buck on the premises, he would be thrown out. He met a couple of guys who were with an orchestra that performed in the club's dining room. One of them, the tenor saxophone player, said he could sort out his immigration papers, but it would cost him. Joaquim didn't have the money, so he robbed the club; he tricked the ageing receptionist with a false alarm. What he got wasn't much, but it covered the saxophonist's fee. The musician pocketed the money and disappeared. It was a hard lesson. Joaquim did not return to the club.

He soon discovered that by assuming an angelic expression he could exploit Americans' sense of charity. He became friendly with a jolly matron from the Salvation Army; he told her that a sax player had stolen his papers, and he was all alone because his mother, the poor dear, had died during the transatlantic crossing. Miss Glitter felt an obstinate, motherly tenderness for him. She went around knocking on doors on his behalf, shouting in high-pitched tones and brandishing her black, worn-out purse like an old suffragette, until she managed to procure his documents.

That's how he was first legally employed, as assistant librarian. Miss Cherney, the head librarian, was skinny as a noodle, all bones and wrinkles. She was going to retire soon, but until then she needed someone to push the book cart for her and climb to the uppermost shelves. It was a boring job. The only patrons were a few old men who probably got in the way at home, and some children whose mothers used the library as a nursery and dumped them there in the afternoon. To kill time, Joaquim took up reading, only adventure novels at first, but then, quite avidly, anything he could get his hands on. It was there at the library, during his time with Miss Cherney, that he learned about radios. He set up a tiny workshop in his rented room, purchased a second-hand radio, procured some spare parts, and began running tests. It was his first apprenticeship, his first real profession.

He became a top-notch technician and soon had his own clients. It was all very timely, for Miss Cherney retired and the young woman who replaced her needed little help and eyed him with haughty indifference, as if watching a line of ants crawling along the grass. In addition to radios, Joaquim repaired irons and toasters. He was quite good at it, and his prices were right. Two years later, his workshop was bringing in a pile of money, provided he worked hard and on his own.

What a shame to have to flee on account of a profitable but not altogether honest business he got involved in. He and his partners, four of them it was, had it all worked out. They held raffles to raise money for destitute orphans who just happened to be imaginary. The prize was a beautiful radio encased in a large frame. They had been running their racket, which was much more lucrative than radio repairs, for nearly six months when they were caught. Joaquim vamoosed, but his colleagues were brought before a judge who was determined to put an end to the juvenile delinquency that plagued New York City's streets in the 1940s. He got out fast, without a penny to his name, and hitchhiked all the way to the West Coast, where he was certain he could start a new life. He was hungry the entire trip and slept rough most of the time. What a big country it was!

Joaquim had just turned eighteen when he arrived in Los Angeles. He met a guy who was pimping out three scrawny girls, the human detritus of the Hollywood dream. Jack had worked in aviation and believed it could be a thriving business if you had the capital to get it off the ground.

They helped each other out, understood each other, and together with two other fellows who were keen on making fast money, they formed a tight-knit group. Joaquim was the one with the smarts and arranged a couple of small-time scams that proved successful. But when one of them got caught, the others, Quim, Jack, and Joseph—a Jew who suffered from tuberculosis—lost heart. Quim set his foot down. Their deals had to be above board, only the rich and powerful could afford to break the law. 'First, we make good honest money,' he said, 'and when we have the capital we need, we go for the big stuff.'

Jack knew about aeroplanes, Joaquim understood radios, and Joseph had some bookbinding knowledge, though not much. They took odd jobs and set up a workshop like the one Joaquim had in New York, but now they also wanted to train as television repairmen. By the end of the forties, the small screen had taken off in the United States, and demand was huge. Bookbinding was the one skill that didn't fit their needs, so while Joaquim specialized in television sets, Joseph focused on antennas.

They succeeded on their own merit. Theirs was not a large workshop, but they put in the time and did a good job on repairs. Jack did the bookkeeping and looked for clients because, as an aircraft mechanic with no official degree, there wasn't much more he could do. When they began to turn a profit, they bought some brand-new TV sets and sold them door-to-door, together with hoovers and lawnmowers. They had no problems before, but now that they were finally making money the quarrels began. In the end, only Jack and Quim stuck it out. Jack thought the time had come to make some quick cash, but Joaquim said: 'No, not yet; be patient.'

One day, they went out to Long Beach to install an antenna at the home of one Jean-Paul Nicolas, who told them he was a French nobleman, though it was plain that he could claim neither of those distinctions. What *was* clear was that the man was filthy rich. He said he wanted to set up a humanitarian organization. He took a liking to them, two young, clever lads who looked like they were down on their luck. He took them under his wing and trained them, and together the three of them founded the society.

Within a couple of years, Joaquim had met all the movers and shakers in Los Angeles and his venture became a proper company. But then Jack decided to go into business on his own and they divided things up amicably. They continued to see each other at the meetings of the society, but it wasn't the same.

Joaquim Simon was a rich man by the time he turned thirty. The more money he made, the more money he attracted. He set aside his plans of joining the criminal class; the field was already saturated, and he had no need to take such risks. He married Melanie Thompson, a pale, blue-eyed girl whose father, the coarse and wealthy owner of a cold-cuts factory, heaved a long sigh of relief and was never heard from again. At forty, having amassed a considerable fortune in liquid assets, he was the owner of a couple of going concerns, and was married to his second wife—Katherine Simpson, the beautiful daughter of a preacher. But Joaquim felt the tug of nostalgia. He couldn't put his finger on the reason, but the truth was he missed home.

He returned to Barcelona in 1970. He did not look for his parents, and no one ever mentioned them. They were probably dead. As for his little sister, there was no telling where she might be. He bought an apartment and made himself known in the circles that mattered. The few nebulous memories he had of the city were like a puff of breath on a cold window, and he had to learn his way around a place that felt foreign. Katherine had no wish to move to Barcelona. The two of them divorced by mail.

That same year of his return from America, he hired a housekeeper, Victòria, who seemed a perfect fit for him. She was impertinent and grumpy, bossy and efficient, and she professed a surly loyalty to him. He travelled a lot, lived discreetly, and adapted to the political changes of the time.

And then, at the age of sixty-four, bored with life and feeling as if there was little left to learn, that skittish, half-wild thing had landed on his doorstep, dispatched from America by his old pal Jack. He embraced the challenge. Here was something he had not attempted before: to raise a girl and make her into something exquisite, a first-rate human being. He had not wanted children from either of his marriages. Yet there he was, bent on transforming Dolores into a delightful creature. Besides, he got a kick out of the wee brat. Playing Pygmalion was a delicate task that required skill and concentration, but from the day Dolores knocked on his door in her filthy rags that reeked of cat piss, Joaquim was never bored again. Now he burned with feeling at night, and his days were filled with yearning. Now, for the first time in his life, his age weighed on him.

CHAPTER III – BOAZ

7
THE THIRD STEP: CHISEL (A)

THEIR RELATIONSHIP CHANGED AFTER THAT DAY AT THE BEACH when Joaquim watched the rain drench Dolores through the restaurant window. They were friends now. Joaquim had felt like a father who unintentionally catches a glimpse of his daughter as she is stepping out of the shower and suddenly realizes that she is no longer a little girl, there can be no more denying that she is a woman now, and so he begins to address her in a different manner, and to treat her as an equal. Seeing her trembling image in the rain he had understood it was time to replace discipline and harsh words with the muted restraint of adult conversation. He gave her a long speech about it, and then he asked if she thought they could be friends.

They now spent long hours in each other's company, laughing and strolling about, buying beautiful things. Victòria spied on them with her small ferret eyes, a trace of fear in her gaze; she kept her mouth shut, but a new kind of wrinkle, long and deep, creased the middle of her forehead.

Joaquim discovered that his charge was greedy and vain and had an overly sweet tooth. If she grew bored, he would suggest going out for ice cream, and then her mood would lighten, and her feet would fly to the door. When she had her fill of sweet things, he would ask if she fancied a new dress, a purse, some shoes, or a dressing gown so diaphanous she would look like an angel walking on clouds. And she would giggle and say *sí*. Sí, sí, sí. She wanted things, she loved them. She pressed them to her chest, then tried everything on—the clothes, the shoes— smiling at her reflection in the mirror, and then at him. Joaquim looked on with detached concentration, as if reading a book.

The change in their routine made her a more attentive student; it was easier for her to learn verb conjugations while strolling and window shopping than bent over a piece of paper, pencil in hand. She no longer looked so wild.

Dolores learned other lessons as well. She discovered some of Joaquim's weaknesses; she knew that when her cheeks dimpled with laughter, or the fiery reflection of her hair, finally long again, flashed across his stern gaze, he could not repress a smile, a faint, muted smile charged with veiled ruminations. Then, like a well-trained pet, he would do as she wished.

'He's proud of me, he really is!' she told Victòria. 'You know what he wants? He wants me to be beautiful! Not strong or clever or cultured or polite, or any of the things he's always talked about. What he really wants is for me to be beautiful. That's what I am to him. Beautiful.' Victòria used a wooden spoon to taste the food that was cooking on the burner, blowing on it some, ignoring the girl's enthusiasm. 'He's spoiling you, is what he's doing,' she told Dolores. 'And I think he's taking it too far.' The food seemed to have a hint of something bitter, as if what Victòria thought but didn't wish to think, what she saw but didn't want to see, what she felt compelled to say but didn't say, had thickened her saliva and dulled her once keen sense of taste.

Joaquim was locked in the bathroom. He had bathed and was now wrapped in a navy-blue terry robe. Having cut his toenails, he sat on the edge of the tub, a round stone bathtub, dark and sensually smooth. With the scissors held flat, he scraped away the dead skin on the soles of his feet. Then he stood before the mirror, rinsed the scissors, and trimmed his bushy eyebrows, which stuck out as if wanting to form a little visor. The wide sleeves of his robe dropped to his elbows, exposing his arms; he saw, at eye level, their reflection in the mirror. They were toned from his daily exercises with resistance bands, but they had liver spots. He didn't trust the mirror, so he held his arms up in front of him. They were full of those hideous freckles, large and pale like coffee stains. Death blemishes. The marks of old age. He looked calmly into the eyes of that other self who lived beyond the mirror and tried to cheer himself up with a smile.

Old age creeps in this petty pace, silently, and just when you think you have chased it away, it strikes with a vengeance. It is the shadow on the wall that relentlessly pursues you. Quicken your step and so too does the shadow. You cannot bargain with it, nor look it in the eye. It is but the meddling of the body with a source of light, you know that, but you cannot escape it or distance yourself, no compromise can be reached. Your only choice is to turn off the light. In the dark, you can pretend the shadow does not exist.

'What a fool you are!' he said aloud. 'Hadn't you decided that you weren't afraid of death?' Maybe Dolores's presence was causing him to lose his bearings. What a shame not to have known her earlier in life. Rubbish, he wouldn't have given that brat the time of day. Certainly, he would never have taken her under his wing or found satisfaction in raising her, adorning her, keeping her well-fed. And he would not have appreciated the kind of beauty that stemmed not from his blood but from his gaze. Would beauty exist without the eyes that recognize it as such?

Joaquim came out of the bathroom feeling downcast, in no mood for games or merrymaking. Dolores tried to convince him to take her to the cinema or window shopping. 'We always have such fun, Quim!' But she could not elicit even a tiny smile from him. 'I'll have dinner in my room, Victòria,' he said. The women glanced at each other and sensed a heavy silence settling on the other side of his closed door, like a stone cleaving the surface of the water. 'He's a lunatic,' Victòria said as she readied his dinner on the footed tray, shaking her head like an empty bucket in the hand of a tired farmer.

Dolores and Jon Carnisser dined alone that night. Quim had forgotten that his friend was coming for supper, and no one mentioned it to him. When Victòria took Joaquim his tray, she found him in bed with his robe still on and his eyes closed. She set the tray on the bedside table and tiptoed out in case he was asleep. He wasn't always pretending.

'Do you think he's cross with me?' Dolores said coyly, wishing to hear her father's friend say that, no, of course not, she was wonderful, and Quim was just being a silly old man.

'He's a little down. Active people get this way from time to time.'

'Active? But he doesn't do anything all day!'

Jon Carnisser leaned back and looked at her with narrowed eyes. The truth was he liked her better when she was half wild. Now she was prim and affected, and her words and gestures rang false. He couldn't fathom why Joaquim thought her so beautiful. She was young and smartly dressed, and she spent long hours grooming herself, but her face was vulgar and plain. The eyes, passable, and her chin was firm, but the curve of her cheeks lacked the soft grace of true beauty. If you took away the acquired refinement, the white blouse with diaphanous bell sleeves, the soft leather belt that wrapped around her waist like a second skin, her black silk trousers, the meticulously dishevelled hair, the manicured daintiness of her hands ... if you removed everything Joaquim had given her and you took the thin, skittish, red-haired girl you were left with and dressed her in cheap clothes, no one would give her a second glance.

Jon was put off by Dolores's affectations, her funny faces, her wolfish self-satisfaction, and he addressed her in the harsh tone that Joaquim had once used with her and he had found so amusing at the time. He told her that if she wished to be a friend to her father, she should behave like one and treat him as an equal, the same way Quim treated her. He said she showed contempt for him and seemed to want to dominate him. He called her perverse. Dolores gave Jon a bored look, and her vacant gaze annoyed him all the more, so he pressed on with his criticism, until finally his words reached that secret place where the skin is so thin that even the flutter of a butterfly's wing causes pain.

She slowly blushed, her eyes filled with tears. She looked at Senyor Carnisser in amazement. He had always been courteous before, so affable and polite. Now he called her selfish, spoiled, insensitive, pompous, stupid. He told her that Joaquim treated her as no one had before, and she was like a doll whose vanity was unjustified. She had been spoiled by the doting affection of a father she did not deserve. In the end, the urge to cry was too much for her. She had been the image of pride, of a self-regard that was steely, iron-clad, diamond-hard, like the sharp glass of a broken bottleneck. But now she jumped up and ran to the kitchen.

Victòria made no attempt to console Dolores; better to shed one's tears: hold them inside and they sour like vinegar. She attended to Jon Carnisser's dinner, moving about in a pleasant, comforting kind of silence. The girl wept quiet tears that fell on her folded hands, and when she stopped crying, she felt calmer, and so very tired.

Victòria was holding the coffee pot when they heard the door slam, and she put it back on the hob. Jon Carnisser would not be tasting the coffee that she was about to serve. He had left the dining room and gone home. Victòria sat down, gasping for breath, and began speaking as if there had been no lapse in their conversation.

'When I was married,' she said, 'my husband and I would sometimes sit together making up stories. We only did this a few times, when the day seemed so long it might never end, and after dinner you found yourself saying, gracious, am I exhausted! We would sit at the round table with the brazier, and I'd make coffee that we sipped very slowly. And suddenly Bernat would say: I found a wallet full of money today, right in the middle of the street, in front of the pharmacy. And I would say: How much was in it? So much he hadn't even had time to count it all. Did you put in in the bank? We had a bank account, and from time to time we put something in for Octavi's studies. Our Octavi was going to grow up to be a proper gentleman, a doctor or lawyer or something along those lines. But money was tight, and we hardly ever made a deposit. Bernat said yes, he had gone to the bank to deposit the money, and the clerk said, wow, fortune has certainly smiled on you! And Bernat told him that he had just won the lottery, and he wanted to keep some cash on him to celebrate, he hadn't given me the news yet ... '

Dolores stared at Victòria mesmerized, her lips parted, her cheeks warm, like a little girl fascinated by a story without knowing quite why.

'He said he left the bank with enough money to buy me a present, it was the teller's idea,' Victòria said.

'But this was all made up? You knew it was just a story?'

'It was a game we played once in a while, when we were dog-tired after a long day ... and so he said he'd come across a young boy who was barefoot and begging on the street, and he'd felt such pity that he'd given him all the money he'd kept. Well done, I said, pleased at this remarkable act of charity. And the wallet? Oh, I gave it to the boy as well. You know what? He looked a bit like our Octavi, and I thought to myself, it's not right for one boy to have so much and another nothing at all ... '

'And you? Did you tell stories as well?' Dolores asked.

'Of course! When he finished his story, I started mine. I told him that a junior lawyer had come to the house and announced that an uncle of mine had passed away in America and left me a beautiful diamond in his will, and it was worth millions because it was one of a kind, there were no other diamonds like it in the whole world. Bernat asked a lot of questions. I told him I had gone to a jewellery store to have it set in a gold tiara, and whatever was left over, all the little pieces, would be for the jeweller, to cover his work and the gold in the tiara. Bernat beamed and said he couldn't wait to see me wearing the tiara … on such days we would go to bed feeling content, as if great things had really happened and justice had been served, for we, by which I mean people like us, deserve good things to happen to us.'

'It seems like a sad story,' Dolores said.

'You're just a silly brat.'

'I know. Father's solicitor made that clear.'

'Good for him.'

'You don't know the things he said to me.'

'Senyor Carnisser? Not half of what I might've told you myself.'

'Maybe.' Dolores rested her head on the palm of her hand and gazed into the distance through a fug of despair. 'But you wouldn't have said it just for the thrill of hurting me.'

That night, she dreamt that Thurber was telling her, Come in, my girl, come inside, so I can pay you for the fridge you found at the dump.

8
THE THIRD STEP: CHISEL (B)

RAMON, THE BREAD BOY, ARRIVED LOADED WITH PARCELS. Victòria wanted to make vol-au-vents. She had ordered a sponge cake and was going to make a filling for it, and the heavy cream Ramon had brought would be whipped into a velvety sauce for the roast beef and mushrooms. In the kitchen, Dolores helped unload all those delicacies that smelled of oven and summer, handling them with great care, as if holding snowballs. Ramon felt intimidated and stared at the floor, at the vol-au-vents, at Victòria.

The wicker basket was empty, the boy had been paid, but he appeared deaf to Dolores's entreaties, so she took his hand and dragged him down the hallway to her bedroom. Like a fly caught in a bell jar, Ramon meekly agreed to sit on her bed and inspected his short black nails with sudden interest.

'What's the matter with you?' Dolores said. 'Aren't we friends any more?'

Ramon lowered his head; certain questions were meant to be heard but not answered.

'Do you still have the lucky charm I gave you?' Dolores used a sweeter, more familiar tone, as if they really were friends.

Ramon nodded. He was upset to feel himself blush; his cheeks burned, those smooth cheeks of his, and yet he was supposed to be a man. Have facial hair. Act grown up. Be tough. Tall, strong, brash. And hairy. Those were the rules. He tugged at the little chain around his neck, the kind that leaves a green mark on your skin, and from inside his jumper appeared the amulet with the splayed spider, looking exactly like it did the first day.

Dolores sighed impatiently; she set about tidying her room to give Ramon time to gather himself. She casually asked him, as if it wasn't a real question, if he wanted to go see the house that was being built on Travessera de Gràcia. It had rained, so they could make little streams and ponds and dams and draw faces with rivulets of dirty water. Ramon looked at her with his mouth agape, like a puppy. She was wearing blue jeans and a yellow sweater that had a crocodile with its jaws open, as if demanding water.

'That's kid's stuff,' he said.

'So what? It's fun.'

'You can splash about right here in your garden.'

There's a cat skeleton buried somewhere. Dig up a dead cat, Dolores, and it comes back to life. It's a bad omen. Cross your fingers and kiss them to ward off the shadow of misfortune.

'Then let's go to the cinema,' she said.

'You and me?'

'Why not?'

'They won't let you go with me.'

What's this all about? Why is he saying that? Is it because he's just a dogsbody for a silly bakery, or maybe because he sees me as the pet that only eats from its master's hand? What do people in the neighbourhood think of me? How do they perceive me? What do they even know about me?

'Are you embarrassed to be seen with me, Ramon?'

The boy pondered the notion of social status, the clout that one gained by becoming a man or stepping out with a rich and beautiful girl on his arm. He grinned.

'Not a chance!' He hesitated for a moment, not knowing what else to say. 'Got any computer games?'

'I don't. And besides, I'd rather go out!'

'Been to the dog races?' His eyes shone with this brilliant idea.

She gave it some thought, knowing she would not be allowed to go. Lately, she had promised herself to behave and be a good daughter to Joaquim. But it wasn't as much fun as it used to be. She looked at Ramon intently and asked him, point-blank:

'What do you think of me?'

'Who, me?'

'Yes, you. You didn't seem to mind playing games before.'

'Kid's stuff.'

'We aren't friends any more?'

'Well, you've changed.'

'Would you please just tell me what you think about me and why you act like I'm a Martian when I'm talking to you?'

'You're *different* now.'

'How so?'

It's not about me being older or looking posh or wearing my nails long and varnished. Ramon says I'm different like it's an insult, he spits it out like a reproach.

'I don't know,' he said. 'Just stuck-up, I guess, like you're better than the rest of us.'

'Me? You're nuts.'

'And also like you've got no … it's like you've lost your strength.'

Dolores tensed up, then coolly left the room. Ramon followed with his head bowed. In the kitchen, Dolores told Victòria to please give *the bread boy* a tip. An eye for an eye: walk all over her and she'd trample him, taunt her and she'd punch back. Ramon smiled and rejected the tip. He gave Dolores a sarcastic look. That's life, Senyoreta: one day you get what you want, and the following day it's someone else's turn. Or how did she think things worked?

Dolores had tonsillitis. She made her convalescence last as long as she could. The white robe she wore was like a cloud, though rather uncomfortable as it caught on everything. She floated about the flat like a sheet ghost, her hair loose, her face scrubbed. She looked like a little girl in fancy dress. Joaquim kept her company the entire time, they talked and talked.

That day they were having breakfast in the kitchen, and Victòria, a tutelary presence, scolded them nonstop. One must guard one's domain or risk invasion by extraneous forces, and that was no way to live, no it was not. Oh, sweet Jesus, how they tried her patience.

'I want to learn to play the piano, Quim!'

'What kind of an idea is that! You want to drive me crazy practicing your scales?'

'Well then, the violin. I'd hold it tight—like this.' Dolores brought her shoulder and chin together, but on her right side instead of the left; she looked rather comical.

'No scales on the violin, huh? What a discovery!'

'You would like that, right? Don't you want me to learn to play an instrument?'

'All right then. I'll get you a harmonica.'

At this, Dolores burst out laughing, and the milk she had in her mouth sprayed everywhere. Nothing was spared: Quim, the table, her own vaporous robe, the decorated tiles that Victòria kept so shiny. Victòria grumbled. Joaquim was happy.

With both hands, you lift the cup to your lips and drink from it. The milk reflects on your skin and gives your cheeks a silvery glow. Still drinking, you open your eyes and look at me, Dolores. You seem to be smiling. In this game of yours, you dip your nose in the white liquid and an explosion of laughter ensues; a thousand droplets splash my face, my chest, my belly. Will I be impregnated by your seminal milk?

Joaquim didn't get Dolores a harmonica or have her take piano lessons. Instead, he said he would teach her to play chess if she wanted; he was sure she would be good, even though everyone knew that women were not gifted at chess. Her reaction to this comment was almost preordained. 'You watch me, just wait and see how I play,' she said boastfully. 'There's nothing a man can do that I can't.' They played every evening, and Dolores was a quick study. Quim wasn't a bad player, but soon he had to give his moves more thought, and he was pleased when he beat her. Dolores was a sore loser, and it was fun to pick on her.

They enjoyed evenings at the theatre and the Liceu Opera House, and they hosted large dinner parties at the flat. He whisked her off to Paris, and she was blown away. If the old gang could see her now! The old gang, to her, meant Colorado Moon, a hard life but solid roots, the place that had forged her and was indelibly seared in her memory. In Paris, she was interested only in art books ('no clothes, Quim, I already have plenty') and in taking a language course. But when they returned home, their living room seemed cold. 'You know what I'd like?' she said. 'A turtle.' They were no trouble at all and beautiful to look at. Victòria was happy to see them again and she acquiesced, but only to a tortoise, those water turtles gave her the creeps.

'Would you say I'm not strong enough, Victòria?'

'Not strong enough? You're starting to sound like him; if you spend all your time together, you'll end up batty too.'

'No, no! It's Ramon, the bread boy, who said it.'

Victòria explained that being strong meant having a certain something inside oneself, though she couldn't really name it or describe what it was. If she lacked strength, it was because she was Senyor's plaything, though she wasn't as silly as she used to be.

Dolores asked Joaquim what she could do to be stronger. He went to the bathroom and brought back his resistance bands. Dolores didn't laugh; she got angry. Quim finally understood what she meant. He sat down in front of her, looked her in the eye, and told her about Ramon's dog.

'He was crushed by a lorry this morning, one of those big lorries,' he said. 'The poor animal was left flat as a pancake. His head was shattered. There was no blood, as if the asphalt had soaked it all up, but the brain splattered everywhere, one eyeball as well. The driver was weeping like a woman as he wiped down the tyres.'

Dolores broke down and started beating Quim on the chest, shouting all the bad words she wasn't allowed to use, cursing in English, out of her mind. He held her by the wrists while she kicked like a wild colt that had never been spurred. He finally released her, and as she stood there panting, he slapped her.

Victòria accompanied her to see Ramon at his home in the neighbourhood of La Verneda. When he saw her, the boy threw his arms around her neck and wept unashamedly. 'I loved him, Dolores!' She hugged him and kissed his short hair, which smelled of cologne. She didn't say anything. Later, at a café, the two of them did their best to get drunk on rum and coke while Victòria sipped absinthe, savouring it, paying no attention to them. 'You're not as posh as I thought, Senyoreta,' Ramon said.

That night, Dolores lay in bed thinking she was not as weak as Ramon thought. She jumped up and grabbed her sketching pad, and she drew a likeness of Tom, the bread boy's lapdog. It turned out well enough, but if you examined it closely, the dog's eyes looked a bit like Quim's.

9
THE FOURTH STEP: QUADRANT (A)

DOLORES WAS NOW FLUENT IN THREE LANGUAGES, SHE HAD read her way through half of Quim's library and had acquired a discerning taste in food and fashion as well as in furniture, not to mention music, art, and theatre. In this time, she had filled out a bit and she was now lovely to behold. She wore black low-cut gowns and kept her hair in a bouffant that ringed her head like a red aura. She could play bridge and golf. And she had mastered the subtle art of conversation. And yet, Victòria said that when she was angry or sad, her secret reservoir of vulgarity surfaced. As always, she was right.

Quim was rejuvenated, he felt ten years younger at least; he took Dolores everywhere and enjoyed showing her off. Jon Carnisser said he envied him a little, it made him regret not having had children. Joaquim swelled with pride, and suddenly he remembered a policeman they had seen in Paris, a traffic officer so full of his own importance that he was a caricature of manhood. He had made Dolores roar with laughter. The two of them still joked about it, and when they wanted to parody authority, they puffed out their chests and raised their heads, blowing an imaginary whistle and waving their arms imperiously.

Joaquim had kidney stones, or at least he had those small, sand-like deposits that precede them. He had a tough time of it, though now he had not only a maid looking after him but also an attentive daughter. When Dolores developed a fever, they wondered if she'd caught it too. Were kidney stones contagious? Victòria had never heard of an empathic disorder, but she was sure that Joaquim had given Dolores his kidney stones. Joaquin poked fun at her.

When the fever had lasted three days, they called the doctor. Ivà Calsina was a close friend of Quim's; he closed the door to Dolores's room and gave her a thorough examination. He was calm when he reappeared. Quim was up, the worst of his kidney attack now over, and he glanced at his friend anxiously. 'It seems she has an infection,' the doctor said, 'but a gynaecologist will need to have a closer look.' He listed half a dozen ailments and identified the likeliest culprit. Joaquim was perplexed.

'Where does it hurt?' Victòria asked the girl.
'Down there. I can't even touch it, it hurts so bad.'
'Is it your belly?'
'Further down.'
'Your bladder?'
'My fanny!'

It was a minor infection, treatable with some honey-coloured vaginal beads. While Dolores dressed, Joaquim grilled the gynaecologist, an eminent physician by the name of Jacint Escrivà.

'But how could she have caught it?'

'Probably at the gym, in the shower or perhaps from a towel, there's no way of knowing for sure. She'll need to take an antibiotic along with this other pill, and she'll be as good as new in a week.'

Joaquim seemed offended that Dolores had vulvitis. A ludicrous name for a humiliating condition. Like having the clap.

'It's just that ... for a girl who has had no carnal knowledge ...' Quim's words sounded revoltingly pompous even to him, but some days you just don't get it right, especially if you are in shock.

The gynaecologist gave him a circumspect look; he scratched his chin, lowered his voice, and stared at the papers on his desk.

'That's got nothing to do with it,' he said. 'Sexual intercourse isn't the only way this can spread. But the thing is, Senyor Simon ... the girl, you see, isn't ... how shall I put it?'

At home, Joaquim shut himself in his study and told Dolores to keep out. He was angry and mortified, like a boy who has failed a test for which he had long been preparing. The following day, he questioned her mercilessly.

'Who did you go with?' he asked with the same expression as that Parisian traffic officer. 'I want to know. I must know! And don't give me any lies because I will crush you like an eggshell. I want the truth!'

It wasn't what he thought, Dolores assured him, feeling insulted and vexed. She stammered and tried not to be confrontational, but he was unrelenting.

'The name. I want the name!'

'Quim, I was raped when I was thirteen. In Colorado Moon.'

She spoke plainly, without theatrics, and her moving frankness had the aura of truth. It drove home the facts. But Joaquim looked her up and down, boiling with anger.

'Who was it?' He suspected her father, there must have been a reason for him to be killed, he was probably a disgusting brute.

'Thurber.'

What a blow. Surely it could not be true, this was twisting the pages of history, this was monstrous. Such a good friend ...

'I've never been with anyone else.'

Just like her father, Joaquim seemed embarrassed to learn that Thurber was a bad person. It was as if he were off-limits, as if she and Thurber were equally to blame for what had happened to her. What a shitty world where male friendship was worth more than a girl's dignity. She didn't matter, only that beastly Thurber mattered. How was this possible?

'Tell me everything,' Joaquim said. 'I want details.'

'I found an old refrigerator at the rubbish tip,' Dolores said. 'It was rusty, but the box itself was intact. Thurber would give me a few dollars for it, if I could manage to move it by myself. If I had to share the money, it wouldn't be worth the trouble. I carried it on my back, and it kept slipping. If I dropped it and it fell apart, Thurber wouldn't want it; he liked things intact, who knew what he did with them later.'

Dolores retold the whole story. The scratch she got on her leg from carrying that piece of junk, the blood that trickled down her calf. Her skinned knees. How she stepped in some dog shit and almost fell, and how she lowered the refrigerator to the ground and wrapped her arms around it to see if it was easier to carry that way. How that thing kept slipping. The perspiration on her temples streamed down her face, droplets of sweat fell as if the refrigerator was weeping. Three times she had to stop to catch her breath. Not much further to go. She tried dragging it, but there were stones and weeds, and the thing refused to budge. When she got to Thurber's store, he took a look at her and then at the fridge.

'You shouldn't play with that,' he said.

'I'm not playing; it's for you. How much do you give me for it?'

'Refrigerators are dangerous, don't you know that? Years ago, a missing boy's body was found inside a fridge that had been left at the tip. You think something that has been discarded is useless, but the door is working so you open it and ... that boy must have climbed inside, and the door closed on him. If you're stuck inside a refrigerator there's no point in screaming. No one will hear you.'

Dolores had never heard old Thurber say so many words, and she showed the kind of impatient respect one has for the elderly. Just bloody pay her and be done with it. Thurber said the refrigerator was in good condition and probably still worked; he'd buy it and use it himself, but she had to help him get it into his home. Home? Yes, of course. Somewhere in that foul-smelling hole was the place he called home. They would have to take it round the back, that's where the bed was, and the kitchenette.

'I was exhausted,' Dolores told Joaquim, 'but he promised me ten dollars, not bad at all, so I helped him. There was a rusty old door at the back. I thought it was no longer in use, but Thurber opened it. It was dark inside, and there was a different kind of bad smell.'

I could hardly see a thing when he closed the door. He threw me on the bed. It was damp, maybe from dew, or sweat, or urine. I don't know. I didn't understand what was happening until he lifted my skirt and started fumbling with my knickers. The gang talked about it. Grownups too. Even I made filthy remarks in jest. I had always thought it was the most disgusting thing humankind had come up with. It was different with dogs, that was something natural ... but to think that one day a man would stick his thing inside me and I might come to like it ... Everyone talked about it, and now that foul-smelling old geezer was on top of me. It was happening. I wanted to scream but he covered my mouth and slapped me. I'm faster than you, I yelled, how dare you, you disgusting pig. I ducked between his legs, trying not to see that horrible thing of his sticking out of his fly, a hard, red thing with a nauseating smell. He removed something shiny from his pocket. At first, I didn't know what it was. I had enough just struggling to get away from that beast. And then I felt it at the back of my neck, hard and sharp. The blade of a knife. My heart stopped. I had to think fast. He won't dare, he won't dare, the bastard is a coward ... and then the tip of that blade pierced my skin, and I was bleeding, and Thurber was tracing a ring around my neck. When the blade touched that vein—what's it called? The one that's so thick that you sever it and it's all over, the one you look for when you want to slaughter an animal. I could feel it throbbing, bulging, and he was going to cut it with that knife. I was very still and waited for him to remove the blade. He ordered me to undress and lie down in a certain way. When he penetrated me, the tip of his knife was on my carotid, yes, I think that's the name, and I was like an ox waiting to be slaughtered. Thurber was panting, but he didn't cut my artery, maybe because I didn't move. I gritted my teeth and endured the pain, the rage, the disgust and humiliation. I felt myself ripping like paper, and there was a searing pain, as if I was being burnt. He released that disgusting liquid and then he withdrew, but I couldn't move. I felt like the dampness of the bed was coming from me, from my own sweat. When I finally left, I couldn't walk straight, my legs were stiff as wood, and there was a thunderclap of pain between them, and blood dripped down my neck.

'He threw me on the bed and raped me right there,' Dolores said.

Joaquim looked sallow. Such things were not meant to be passed on; it was torment to hear her account, it was as if he had also been raped. Dolores felt a twinge of compassion.

Joaquim gritted his teeth. 'You slut,' he said. 'You animal. Why didn't you defend yourself?' As he spoke, some of his saliva landed on Dolores's face. Then he struck her furiously.

CHAPTER IV - VISIT

10
THE FOURTH STEP: QUADRANT (B)

SHE AWOKE WITH A START, AS IF HER SLEEP HAD BEEN RENT. Covered in sweat, Dolores sat up in bed. There was Joaquim, visible in the dim light of the streetlamp, his round eyes watching her. It scared her to death. 'What are you doing here?' she said. Joaquim told her she had been screaming; he came to check on her and saw that she was asleep, but he stayed in case she felt unwell. Dolores was disturbed by the thought of being watched while she slept.

Dolores had been quite ill, and the antibiotics were not working. Joaquim told her to her face that he found her revolting. She was so despondent that it triggered a fever. For ten days her body and spirit were wracked with aches and pains.

Victòria would have said it was a good sign that Joaquim had checked on her when he heard her screaming in her sleep. Maybe he was softening a bit. Maybe he was starting to understand. Or forgive. Forgive *what*? Why did *she* need forgiveness? Or were victims the offenders now, and wrongdoers the affronted party?

But Joaquim had not heard her cry out, nor did he harbour any sense of compassion, or forgiveness or magnanimity, nothing of the sort. He often entered her room at night, cautiously, a shadow in the dark, and he gazed at Dolores for a long time. He never tired of it. Watching her sleep was the best moment of his day. That night, tall Joaquim, white-haired Joaquim, whose receding hairline made him look distinguished, had been aroused during his vigil. Beads of sweat formed on his forehead, there was a warm sensation in his hands and belly. He looked at Dolores like a hungry man contemplating his dinner, and he masturbated in the unbroken silence, his eyes on her, and with each wave of pleasure he could almost feel Dolores's skin, touch it, bite into it, although it was only his own lips that he was biting. He didn't let out a sigh, but his chair made a little squeaking sound. And as the greatest pleasure overtook him and he was stunned at the joy of his solitary act, at that precise moment Dolores woke up, as if she had somehow shared in his hidden pleasure, as if he had filled her with his secret desire, so well hidden beneath layers of paternal indifference. He had just enough time, in that instant when Dolores passed from sleep to wakefulness, to cover himself and hide his throbbing member under his red silk robe.

The following day they seemed to have made their peace. He felt guilty, and so did she. Each would have liked to be absolved by the other. This brought them closer, like two people walking together, one lame, the other blind, each needing the other.

For dessert, Victòria served sliced kiwis sprinkled with sugar and drowned in church wine. Dolores, who still didn't have an appetite, stirred the wine with a spoon and listlessly poked at the sliced fruit. 'They look like eyes, don't they, Quim? Eyes that are watching me.' Joaquim looked at the thin, delicate slices, but he didn't see any eyes. He saw a neat line of black dots tracing an oval surrounded by green. The centre was white. He saw the cavity through which life comes into being, and his wild thoughts returned to the solitary pleasure he experienced as he watched Dolores sleep. He eagerly bit into the fruit.

Victòria and Dolores took the bus home. The girl had been well enough to visit the gynaecologist. He gave her the all-clear, she was cured, and he prescribed some tablets to bring a bit of colour to her sallow cheeks. The doctor and nurse had both been in the room as Dolores undressed, but when she was about to lie down on an examination table that had two stirrups for her legs, a young man entered. 'My son,' the doctor said, and he let him peer into Dolores's mauve-coloured cavity. The young man, who was about her age, was hunched over with embarrassment as he examined her in all her female nakedness. Dolores wanted to die. She wanted to close her legs. The father turned on a lamp, revealing all her secrets, as if she was just a worthless insect. When they were done, the boy helped her up, and he and Dolores glanced at each other with what seemed like a bolt of light and confusion. Seeing the doctor's son looking so uncomfortable made her feel a bit stronger.

On the bus ride home, the two women were silent. All at once Dolores said: 'He won't let me go anywhere by myself, Victòria. And I'm eighteen years old. *I think.*' This qualification was soft enough to be inaudible. She repeated it silently to herself. I think, I think, I think. Like an insect buzzing in her head.

'I had an abortion,' Victòria said. 'Octavi was seven years old, and I never thought I would have another child.'

I did it myself, with a knitting needle that I dipped in boiling water, like I had been told to do. When I realized that I was dying, I screamed from the bed where I was bleeding out. Octavi was at school, and Bernat had died the month before. I couldn't have a child, not alone, not without Bernat! I couldn't. I did the bit with the needle, and the blood gushed out. Somehow, I managed to open the window, hoping that Quimeta, the neighbour upstairs, would hear me. She did, and she called a doctor. He sent for the fire brigade, so they would kick down my door. I was almost unconscious by the time the doctor got to me. The blood had soaked through the mattress, I could hear it dripping onto the floor, plink, plink, plink. I was getting drowsy. I wanted to let go, to give up. But I had Octavi to think about. I couldn't die. An ambulance was called. When I recovered, the doctor told me he wouldn't report me, he understood what had happened; a pregnant widow was something else altogether, there was no sin in what I had done. When I returned home, I went up to Quimeta's flat to collect Octavi, and he hugged me so tightly that I regained the will to live, and then ...

'I got pregnant and had an abortion,' Victòria said. 'I nearly bled to death. I was treated by a doctor whose name was Jacint, like your doctor. Isn't that a coincidence?'

Quim was excited when they got home; he had a surprise for Dolores. 'To celebrate your recovery,' he told her, 'and so you'll see that I don't hold a grudge.' Victòria was taken aback; she didn't know what they were talking about, and she was used to always being in on things. It put her in a bad mood to be left out. 'It's in my study,' Quim said. 'The surprise. I think you're going to love it.' When he said *I think,* Dolores again heard that think, think, think reverberating in her brain like a thousand buzzing insects. Quim followed her into the study, eager to see her reaction.

There was a basket on the table, a wicker basket with two flaps that opened outwards. Inside was a little puppy. It was a Bracco Italiano, cream coloured with black spots, not a month old. Dolores lifted it with clumsy hands, trying not to squeeze it or hurt it. The creature shivered with cold. She hugged it to her chest, and the puppy stirred, seeking air and freedom. Dolores didn't say anything. She ran to the kitchen to look for milk. Victòria stared with surprise at the tiny bundle of life in the girl's arms, and then, almost without thinking, she started heating some milk.

They tried to force the puppy to taste it, but it didn't want the milk or didn't know how to drink it. All it did was tremble and look pitiful. 'Poor thing! Poor thing!' Victòria fashioned a nipple out of cloth, improvising a baby bottle, and it did the trick. Dolores held the puppy to her chest and suckled it with the milk-soaked cloth. She felt as if she were nursing the puppy from her own body. Then she gently placed it at the foot of the stove and frantically searched the kitchen for something soft on which to lay the dog. She still hadn't opened her mouth. 'Simmer down, girl,' Victòria said, 'be patient!' She found an old blanket and cut it into strips, and they made a bed for the puppy, which they placed by the radiator in the hall. They petted the dog, though Victòria was grumbling.

The blood had drained from Dolores's cheeks; it was plain that this was the most precious gift she had ever received. Quietly thrilled, she gazed at the puppy, not really hearing Victòria's false lamentations: 'They are a lot of work, dogs are, running about all day long, and in the end, mark my words, who will clean up after it, feed it and walk it? Poor old Victòria, that's who! It's easy to want a dog when someone else is doing the drudge work of looking after it. I thought we had agreed there would be no animals. I made that clear the first day I started here. At most we discussed a turtle. And now, lo and behold, here we have it—a dog. The masters' whims are the law of the land, and if anyone has a problem with that, well, they'll just have to suck it up, won't they?' But Victòria was smiling at the puppy as she was saying this, adjusting the blanket around it to make it comfortable. 'You can tell he misses his mother, the wee darling.'

Dolores raced around the flat like a maniac, as if the dog might vanish if she let it out of her sight. She searched the place until she found the old breadbasket, and she lined it with another bit of blanket. Then Victòria helped her make a litter box, fortunately they had some sawdust in a sack that was stored in the tool cupboard, left over from when the rain had seeped through the back door to the gallery. They finished the litter box and talked about raising a well-behaved puppy. Dolores was shocked to hear Victòria say that the thing to do when a dog doesn't obey is, wham, smack its backside and see if that doesn't help. It's only an animal. But Victòria's expression was gentle. Dolores looked lovingly at the sleeping puppy and said they would need to get a book about dog care and learn all about vaccines and everything else. 'Nonsense,' Victòria said, stroking the puppy with a tenderness that was as palpable as the window she had just wiped.

Almost an hour had passed since Quim had led Dolores into his study to give her his surprise, and she still hadn't thanked him. Now she gazed at him with infinite gratitude and fondness, her wide blue eyes filled with wonder. She threw her arms around his neck and kissed him on the cheek. Her child-like enthusiasm was moving. 'I love you more than anything in the world, Quim!' she said.

11
THE FIFTH STEP: LEVEL (A)

A BOUQUET OF FLOWERS ARRIVED FOR DOLORES. IT WAS FROM the doctor's son. His name was Jacint, just like his father, and like the doctor who stanched Victòria's desperate bleeding many years before. It came with a card.

Congratulations on your recovery.
Jacint Escrivà Jr.
 P.S. Don't think doctors are always this thoughtful, but I must try to keep my father's patients as best I can. The flowers are a bribe.

The bouquet of tulips and daisies was beautiful, and Dolores laughed as she held it up. Then she handed it to Victòria and asked her to put it in a vase. What a nice young man! A spark of restlessness fluttered in Dolores's stomach as she recalled being intimately exposed to the young man's scrutiny, but then she forgot about it and started playing with the puppy. She did little else besides spoiling that puppy. She took him to the vet and fed him with loving obstinacy. She never left him alone. The dog was a bit overwhelmed by all the attention. 'I want Ramon to see him, but I'm not sure what to do,' she said. 'What do you think, Victòria? And you, Joaquim? Maybe it will make him sad because he'll be reminded of his poor Tom ... but what shall we name him? It has to be a pretty name, but it should be, I don't know, very—'

Joaquim had eyed the bouquet like a man discovering a beetle in his bed, but now, seeing the girl so wrapped up in the dog—*her* little dog—he remembered his manners and social obligations. He wanted to set a good example. 'You must thank this young man,' he said.

Dolores rose early, as soon as she heard the dog barking. She took better care of him than one would a baby, but she stayed in her robe all day, her hair dishevelled, all her attention on the pet. If she didn't shape up, Victòria told her, she would kick the stupid dog, he was driving her crazy. Dolores blanched at the threat. Joaquim listened to this exchange with a stony smile on his face. Either you do this and that and the other or I'll beat the dog, he imagined himself saying. For that matter ... I could always just kill it. He dismissed this thought as the logic of a thug; becoming a gentleman had been hard work.

The surly neighbours on the third floor complained that they couldn't get a proper night's rest because of that insufferable puppy and its incessant yapping and whimpering. They sent their maid down, an older woman like Victòria who had only been working for them for a short while. She was lanky, with prominent cheekbones that were like two bumps, and a snub nose. She spoke with the meek politeness of common people. If it wasn't too much to ask, if they would be kind enough to put themselves in their shoes, and so on. Victòria said that the lady and gentleman upstairs should also try to understand the situation; keeping a puppy quiet was no easy feat, but they grew fast, and theirs was going to be a well-behaved dog that never barked. And then they would see the benefits of having a dog in the building. It would help keep thieves away. Thieves shared information and told each other everything. Didn't she know that they left scratch marks by the doors that were like a secret code? And where there was a mentally handicapped person living, they made a mark with their knife so no one would rob that family. Sometimes hoodlums are more humane than gentlemen, you see.

The maid from upstairs must have been given specific instructions. She spoke with a Galician accent, and her humble demeanour belied the fact that she was tough as nails. Victòria's words did nothing to impress her. She insisted that her employers were thinking of going to the police, and ... Dolores flew into a rage and started cursing at her. The woman stepped back and made her case a bit more meekly, but Dolores rushed up the stairs to the third floor, her robe floating behind her like a paper butterfly, and she started pounding on the neighbours' door. Joaquim appeared when the shouting began, but with Victòria hot on Dolores's heels there was no time to restore order or tell Victòria to put a stop to the girl's outburst. She caught up with Dolores at the precise moment that the cat-eyed Senyora from upstairs opened her front door. Victòria grabbed Dolores by the arm and dragged her back down to the apartment. 'More than all you lot, you horrible people, you beasts!' Dolores was shouting. 'My dog is worth more than you and all your rotten family.' Joaquim slapped her. Dolores fell silent and lowered her head as if exhausted, but she didn't cry. She was quiet, her head bowed, her chest rising and falling like a windsock.

'I'm sorry I lost my temper.' She raised her head and looked at Joaquim. 'But don't ever hit me again.'

'I will do so as often as I like,' Joaquim told her. 'Understood? Your language, Dolores, your manners ... you know I detest rudeness! You were born vulgar and that's how you were raised, and all I can do is give you a coat of varnish. But it doesn't take much to awaken the animal in you.'

Dolores didn't speak for the rest of the day; she locked herself in her room with the dog and emerged only to get food for her puppy. She didn't eat a thing. Joaquim paced the living room as Victòria addressed him in a cloying tone, as if he were ill.

Joaquim was having supper when the girl appeared at the door holding the dog in her arms.

'I have a name for him,' she said. 'I'll call him Vulgar.'

'That's an ugly name, Dolores. It doesn't suit him at all.'

'I know, but it makes him mine.'

Holding his spoon aloft, Joaquim nodded and continued eating. The television was broadcasting news of people being killed all over the world. Dolores put the dog in his basket, turned off the TV, and sat down next to Joaquim.

'May I have my dinner? I'm hungry.' Without waiting for an answer, she dipped his dessert spoon in his soup and tasted it. She smiled. 'Yummy!'

Victòria was already standing by the table with extra cutlery and another bowl of soup. She scolded Dolores for wearing her bathrobe all day and for being so rude. 'Who ever heard of dunking a spoon in another person's bowl?' she said. 'Is that what you've learnt here, Senyoreta? Not even a saint would have the patience that is required of me!'

The scolding was meant to appease Joaquim. He knew this, Dolores knew this, and Victòria knew that everyone else knew this.

'It's because of the dog, can't you see?' Dolores said. 'I wanted one so badly, you can't imagine! That's why I lost it earlier and talked back to you; it's why I don't get dressed and don't go out. But I'll get used to the dog, to Vulgar. When I told you that I love you so much, I really meant it, Quim. I don't deserve you. Please forgive me.'

'That's rich!' Victòria served Dolores a piece of breaded hake with a lemon wedge and a sprig of parsley. 'So, that's it? Sorry and it's over and done with and you can start over? What have I done to deserve this?'

Joaquim reached across the table for Dolores's hand and smiled at her with paternal magnanimity.

'Starting tomorrow,' Dolores said, 'I'll get up early and get dressed, walk Vulgar and study hard. Oh, and I must phone the doctor's son. I haven't thanked him for the flowers. Or would it be better to send a note, Quim?'

The fingers squeezing Dolores's hand went limp, and Joaquim's fatherly smile vanished like a light bulb that had just burned out. He ate his fish and grumbled about a fishbone being stuck in the roof of his mouth.

You stood at the window, and I was nowhere, I was far from your mind. You had just woken up, your hair was messy, your lips pale. The dawn gazed upon you with pleasure, and the rising sun mirrored the incandescence of your hair.

12
THE FIFTH STEP: LEVEL (B)

IF THE GRAND ARCHITECT OF THE UNIVERSE HAS GIVEN THEE a son be grateful unto Him, but tremble for the deposit which He hath confided to thy care; be unto such child the living image of divinity; cause him up to ten years of age to fear thee; up to twenty to love thee, so that even until death he may respect thee. Even up to ten years of age be his Master, to twenty years of age his father, until death his friend; strive to teach him good principles rather than fine manners, so that he may owe thee an enlightened and upright understanding, rather than a frivolous elegance; and make an honest man rather than an able one.

—Masonic Code of Ethics

Ramon finally came to meet Vulgar. He bluntly told Dolores that she was doing a terrible job of raising him; he would turn out spoiled and whiny. It would have been better to get a silly lapdog than a noble animal like that.

'Dogs don't need to be petted in order for them to love you,' he said.

'But he's so soft!'

'Bollocks, he's a dog! He needs to be fed and walked, to be vaccinated and taught to do his business in his litter box. He's not a toy. What's wrong with you!'

Ramon's criticism made more of an impact than any of Victòria's sermons.

Dolores and Ramon had decided to go to the cinema. Joaquim gave them some money to stop at a café after the film, he told Dolores that he was pleased she was going out with Ramon. 'I detest the kind of snob that wouldn't give Ramon the time of day,' he said. 'You mean like the family on the third floor?' Dolores said, and they both laughed. That night Dolores didn't give the dog a single kiss, and the dog didn't appear to miss it. From then on, she tried to do what was expected of her. She got dressed in the morning and looked after Vulgar without smothering him with love. She helped Victòria, though behind Joaquim's back. And she studied hard.

Young people, the sons and daughters of friends, began to attend Joaquim Simon's soirées and dinner parties. Dolores was happy about this. Hosting others was an honour, and it meant that now she had some normal people to talk to, even if the conversation was more often a group discussion and flowed smoothly. One young man, Serafí Renom, suggested an outing to the seaside to try out his new motorboat; they'd go up to Roses and then take the boat out and go to l'Escala. The son of a banker, Serafí was a handsome and well-bred young man about town who had a reputation for being friendly. His sister, Roser, would be joining them, as well as Martí, the son of Domènec Vives, who had been in textiles and now owned a casino. 'What about us adults, can't *we* come?' said Senyor Vives, more in jest than expecting an invitation. Serafí apologized but explained that this wouldn't be possible. 'I've just got my captain's licence and don't have much practice yet,' he said, 'so I can't take more than three or four people. But you, Dolores, absolutely. We'll have a wonderful time. The weather's perfect! I can't wait to take the boat out for the first time. We can all have dinner at Motel when we get back. Martí, shall we take your car or mine?'

Dolores, one eye closed, held her glass up to the light, as if the whole thing had little to do with her. The boys were making plans without even thinking to ask if she wanted to go. They took it for granted. Joaquim pushed back his chair; his face was in the dark, and he gazed at Dolores not knowing whether he was pleased about these plans or just the opposite.

'So, what do you think?' he asked Dolores. The question was posed openly but in an intimate tone.

Dolores's response was meant only for Quim. 'I'm not keen on it. I've made plans with Ramon. That is, if you agree to lend us your computer. He really wants to show me some of his new computer games.'

'Where does he get all these computer games? They're not cheap,' Joaquim said, as if wanting the others, who were half-listening, to know they were talking about a boy who came from modest means and they'd feel superior. It was just the kind of thing Joaquim would do.

'Sant Antoni market; there's a swap meet on Sundays. They exchange stuff.'

'Exchange? That doesn't sound legal to me.'

'So what? Why shouldn't Ramon have computer games if he likes them so much?'

Everyone heard this and they were all silent, a charitable smile on their faces; some questions aren't meant to be answered, it would be in poor taste. It was obvious, no? In life, there were the haves and the have-nots, it had always been this way, and since not much could be done about it, there was no point in getting worked up. Then Joaquim brought out his box of Cohiba cigars and a fine cognac that he saved for special occasions. He puffed out his chest and patted his stomach. You might say he was euphoric.

Dolores declined the boys' invitation, but they insisted, so she promised to join them the next time.

'This Sunday won't work for me. I've already made plans.'

'Bah!'

But she didn't back down.

The following day, when Victòria took Joaquim his breakfast in bed, she had things to say. Her rambling account followed the usual tedious path, which Joaquim endured because it meant Victòria had something to tell him, and when Victòria had something to say, it was always a good idea to listen. She told him that she had run into the maid from upstairs, the scrawny woman with high cheekbones and a Galician accent that gave her voice a whimpering cadence ... and here Victòria got a little sidetracked talking about the Galicians she had met and how hardworking they were, although you never knew what they would do next, but good people on the whole, yes indeed, and in Galicia they understood the meaning of hard work, especially the women, it was so unfair, all the men leaned on them, the lazy lot. Me? Give me a Galician woman, the men you can toss into the sea ... Finally, Victòria came round. The upstairs maid had told her that, a week ago, Dolores had gone up to their flat and asked to see the Senyora, though this wasn't something Severina, for that was the name of the maid on the third floor, had overheard herself, she was busy enough as it was, cleaning up after everyone, like most of us in this line of work, always tidying up the mess that the masters leave behind—'

'Prou!' Joaquim said. 'Enough, Victòria! What the bloody hell did Seferina or Sefarina or whatever she's called, the maid upstairs, tell you?'

'So, who's foul mouthed now?' Victòria said. 'If the girl swears, she gets a telling off. Where do you think she gets it from? She didn't learn it from me, that's for sure, and whatever bad language she uses in English I couldn't care less about. I don't understand it, so it's in one ear and out the—'

'For heaven's sake, woman, just spit it out!'

'Well, Dolores went to see the Senyora, and she asked her, very politely, like a true Senyoreta, to please forgive her. She said she was recovering from a fever and the medication she was on was affecting her nerves; the last thing she wanted was to offend anyone, least of all her third-floor neighbours, who were such good neighbours; it was a real pleasure to have them upstairs. Those were her words. I have to say that I felt as proud as if she were my own. The girl has these outbursts. One day you would strangle her, the next day you would smother her with kisses. But if I were you, I would keep quiet. If she hasn't mentioned it, then it's her business, and it's clear that she didn't do it to score any points but because she meant it.'

Dolores spent the afternoon in the kitchen making little tuna cakes that Victòria declared tastier than the ones from the pastry shop. She wanted to impress Ramon. If he knew she'd made them herself he'd poke fun at her, but he'd be pleased. Victòria did most of the work, but surely Dolores's good intentions counted too. Joaquim, who'd been out, arrived while they were still in the kitchen. Thank goodness he was in good spirits. He stuck his head round the door, smiled, and asked if this was one of those times when he was barred from the kitchen and had to pretend that Dolores wasn't really in there helping out. With that, he headed to the living room.

Dolores went back to her room to comb her hair and found a brand-new computer on her desk. It had even been plugged in. The blue screen was flashing, as if impatient for Ramon and Dolores to start playing on it. The shrieks of joy she let out brought Victòria running. The woman wrung her hands over the extravagance. Why would they want another computer when they already had one? It was plain lunacy. She turned around contemptuously and retreated to the kitchen, the only place where order and common sense prevailed.

'Quim! Quim! You're the best!'

Joaquim removed Dolores's arms from around his neck and told her, with feigned sternness, not to think that everything could be bought with a few kisses. He had been made aware of certain things and was glad to do that for her. He meant the gift. He said he was proud of her, though he struggled to get the words out. Dolores covered her mouth with her hands and danced around him, jumping up and down, tousling his hair from behind his armchair. Joaquim didn't have the heart to scold her; instead, he sweetly asked her to leave. He remembered how Jon had taunted him when he asked him to keep the new computer a few days.

On the little balcony off Joaquim's bedroom, the pot that once held the wall germander looked lonely, the plant had succumbed to the winter. Now the empty pot seemed old and dusty, and as cold as the bare and lifeless earth inside it.

After playing video games, the two young people decided to try a new pizzeria where they piled their pizzas high with melted cheese. From the balcony, Joaquim watched them leave the building, their turned backs moving away down the street, their young silhouettes so vital, as if filled with swarming insects. He felt left out and melancholy. Suddenly, his whole body stiffened. Ramon must have just said something that annoyed Dolores, and she had kicked his backside, a gesture Joaquim deplored and found extremely vulgar. He smiled bitterly and lowered the blinds.

When Dolores returned, she found Joaquim asleep in front of the television, a pornographic film flashing before him in technicolour.

CHAPTER V – INTERIORA

13
THE SIXTH STEP: PLUMB LINE (A)

'SHORTLY BEFORE I RETURNED HOME TO BARCELONA,' QUIM said, 'I met a boy who had been born blind. This was the 1970s, around the time when Uri Geller was a media sensation. You know who Uri Geller was?'

'The name rings a bell,' Dolores said.

'I'm sure it does; he was quite famous. The man could bend spoons.'

'What the—I can do that too!'

'You're so clueless, Dolores!' Quim said. 'Uri Geller bent them through the television. I mean that when he came on his programme spoons in people's homes would bend. Broken clocks would start ticking. And some black and white television sets suddenly transmitted in full colour. That's what people said, everyone talked about it. But later he was revealed as a con artist, and that was the last anyone ever heard about him.'

'But did you see it?' Dolores said. 'Did your spoons bend when this Uri appeared on-screen?'

'God forbid! I never watched his programme. But it's a bit like Caroline of Monaco; even if you weren't interested, you still heard about it all the time. This sort of thing drew a huge audience back then. Today too, I imagine. And besides, they always trotted out one scientist or another to impart credibility on the whole thing and make it seem plausible. There are good scientists and bad scientists, you know, just like there are good and bad taxi drivers or accountants, the only difference being that when the word *scientist* is attached to a name or a face, apparently the only thing to do is say *amen*. Uri Geller's case, like so many others, ended as these things do—abruptly. Suddenly it's over and no one mentions it again. Radio silence. *C'est fini*. The end. Well, one night I was after some entertainment and headed to the Imperial Theatre in Los Angeles, and this blind boy was on the show. He had psychic powers. The playbill gave an account of his life. When he was little, eight or maybe even ten years old, he told his mother that he could see a dot of light. The boy had been blind all his life, and the mother, hearing about this dot of light, got her hopes up and went to see the head of ophthalmology at the hospital.'

'The head of what?' Dolores said.

'Good grief, you really are an ignoramus! *Ophthalmos* means *eye*, and *logos*, something like *treated*, more or less, so therefore ... '

Joaquim couldn't stop himself from playing the teacher.

'Oh, an eye doctor!' Dolores said.

'The boy's mother insisted that her son, Sasha Moore was his name, could see. At least a little. The ophthalmology department took an interest in his case and ran lots of tests, but nothing doing. The boy's optic nerve was damaged, and that's no joke, there's no fixing that. But the boy insisted he could see a tiny dot of bluish light.'

'How could a blind person know the light was blue? I mean, how can a blind person know what blue is?'

'Indeed,' Quim replied. 'And how could he know what a dot of light was? What concept did he have of that? He knew the word of course, but what idea did it correspond to? Do we think in concepts, or do we think in words? A word is a concrete thing with a certain sound and spelling, but what about a concept? How is it acquired or formed? What is the concept of *dot of light* for someone who was born blind? Such things have no answer, or they shouldn't, I say, but I'm an old sceptic who doesn't believe in much, and I say it's better to let sleeping dogs lie. Otherwise, you end up going mad.'

'So, what happened?'

'The doctors asked Sasha's mother to write down the exact time the bluish dots appeared, and their frequency. And the mother told her son to let her know whenever he saw them, even if Sasha insisted that the light lasted less than a second. It turned out it was always at night, when it was completely dark in the room, and he was in bed half asleep. In other words, there was no chance of there being any light at all. It happened in the dark and lasted less than a sigh. The boy said he had to concentrate hard to make the light appear. Though the doctors dismissed any possibility of recovery, the mother clung to hope. And then a television producer put Sasha in contact with some psychics who were entertainers, and they trained the boy. He went into show business, divining people's thoughts and finding hidden objects and other such nonsense.'

'Are these things ever real?' Dolores said.

'No, my girl, never! If any of it were true, it wouldn't be a show, never doubt that. The innocent is innocent because he doesn't know that he is, or he wouldn't be innocent at all. See what I mean?'

'What happened then?'

'Well,' Quim said, 'I had nothing else to do that day, so I went to the theatre and watched his show. He was about twenty at the time, and I had already made up my mind to return to Spain. For some reason, I was homesick. Imagine missing a place you can hardly remember ... we are pure biology, Dolores. The place where we spend our formative years is part of our biological memory, it has nothing to do with patriotism or any of that rubbish.'

'I remember less and less of my country,' Dolores said.

'That's because you're young; we'll talk about it again when you're forty. That show with the blind boy didn't interest me at all, but then I saw him clowning around pretending to concentrate and all that foolishness, and he just seemed so despondent. He looked like a victim of a nasty scheme.'

'Scheme? Whose scheme?'

'His mother's, for one. Mothers are a curious specimen; they are capable of killing for their children, everyone knows that, and some will even kill their own children. Out of love, of course, as hard as that is to understand. If an entrepreneur or producer takes an interest, the child is doomed. For that kind of attention, a mother will sell her soul to the devil. Her child's success is worth more than money, it's a payment on an unnamed debt that she cannot forgive. Or maybe it's how she plans to convince the world that she birthed a unique individual. Mothers are the bane of the entertainment industry, mythical creatures, pure literature and vitriol! In my opinion, they just lose their minds and project everything onto ... Oh, I don't know. The thing is, I was moved by that poor boy who pretended to guess people's names and ages and the money that audience members had in their pockets. He was pale and emaciated, not much fun to watch. I felt terrible for him. After the performance, I went to see him. He was sitting alone in the semi-darkness of his dressing room, smoking a menthol cigarette with his makeup still on. Perhaps he was waiting for his doting mother to come and help him change. How strange life is!'

'But why did you go to see him?' Dolores asked.

'Maybe to keep him company, maybe to help him.'

Soon I would be returning home, and I had something I didn't want to throw away or take with me. It was an encumbrance. Who could keep it for me? There was no one I trusted enough, and I didn't know anyone who was oblivious to the significance of the object. It had to be a stranger, so if it was stolen or thrown away, I would feel no regret because I would never find out. I couldn't get rid of it entirely because it held meaning for me. Sasha was the perfect person, and when I asked him to keep it, he seemed grateful.

'I acted on impulse,' Quim said. 'I told him he was being exploited by a bunch of scoundrels who were taking advantage of a special talent he didn't even possess. No one does. He smiled faintly and looked like a tormented ghost who had held that same thought every minute of every day. I told him that if he did me a favour, I would pay for him to attend a school for the blind. Believe it or not, he couldn't read or write; he'd just never got around to it, he explained. They are like vultures, mothers are, if they think there's something in it for them. I knew of a good school right there in Los Angeles. I gave him the address and a good bit of money. I told him to run away, there and then. In exchange, I asked only that he keep something for me.'

'What was it? What was he supposed to keep for you, Quim?'

'None of your concern.'

'Shit. You can't leave me like that!'

'Language, Dolores! How many times do I have to tell you?'

'Oh, but you're allowed to use bad words, right?'

'It's different.'

'My foot.'

'The boy took my hands and tried to thank me, but I would have none of it.'

'You're a fucking hero.'

'I'm no hero, certainly not a fucking hero, and I'm going to wash out your mouth with soap, young lady.'

'Did he? Run away? Did he learn to read and write?'

'I don't know,' Quim said. 'I didn't tell him my name, or how to find me. You know what? This is the first time I've shared this with anyone. For all I know, he's still doing his act.'

'And did he keep that thing for you?'

'I don't know.'

'In my opinion, asking him to hold on to something for you was just a way of hiding the fact that you were doing him a favour, and convincing him it was a tit-for-that, one favour for another. Like I said, you're a f— ... guy ... hero ... what's a synonym for the f-word?'

Joaquim shooed Dolores away and stayed in his study by himself. He remembered the medallion as if it were right in front of him. A triangle, and inside the triangle something that looked like the coat of arms of the city of Valencia: four red bars topped by a crown between two columns. The columns were Ls with their backs to each other. Beneath was another triangle circumscribing an eye and a square surrounded by rays of light. He truly loved it! But breaking old bonds means just that, breaking old bonds. And then, from the far corners of his memory, everything resurfaced in the wake of Jack Thurber's letter, those four scribbled lines, and Dolores's arrival.

Joaquim tried resting his eyes and conjuring a bluish dot of light. Sometimes it worked. But he wasn't blind.

The past has a way of doing this from time to time, it breaks through. And then that moment is again in front of you, almost tangible. Why do we remember so many things? Or better still: why do we forget them?

14
THE SIXTH STEP: PLUMB LINE (B)

DOLORES PERSUADED VICTÒRIA TO GO TO THE HAIRDRESSER. She had discovered that Victòria dyed her hair with a dribbly black liquid that gave it a fake, glazed effect, kind of like Chinese lacquer. She hadn't mentioned this to her because Victòria liked to boast that, at sixty, she didn't have a single grey hair. You looked at that big woman and wondered how there could be any vanity hidden beneath all those layers of ugliness. Maybe when we look in the mirror, the image we see is softened by our fierce self-regard.

To convince Victòria to go, Dolores told her that wearing her hair slicked back wasn't stylish and it made her look older. The hairdresser could give her a perm as soft and velvety as a wind-stirred field of wheat. 'They could even dye your hair while we're there,' Dolores said. 'Not that you need it, but a lighter shade of black would soften your features.'

The corners of Victòria's mouth drooped with distrust. She felt disdain for the unnatural things people did to mask their appearance, and she was reluctant to being scrutinized by vapid young girls she didn't know and groomed in front of those large, brightly lit mirrors that were so unforgiving. But she acquiesced. Quim saw Dolores gesturing at him, and he refrained from teasing Victòria; he saw them off with a smile that seemed to be stifling a chuckle. The whole thing was a joke, and Victòria let it be known that she was only going to the hair salon to silence Dolores, that annoying little brat who was always on about her hair. But even as she said this, she blushed.

Vulgar had grown a lot and was an obedient dog now; he was still a puppy, and quite playful, but he was also well behaved. More so than most people. He knew how to act around the mistress, the master, and the servant, and he never got it the wrong way round. Alone with Quim, Vulgar resisted the urge to play. He lay on the carpet at his master's feet like an old dog, very still, but he wagged his tail. Quim didn't even glance at him, but when he began to speak out loud, the puppy raised his head and paid attention. He was the colour of burnt milk, and his spots, much like Dolores's freckles, had lightened over time. The tip of his tail was white, his snout black, his eyes dark and shiny, and moist like two large drops of black water. Quim stood up, and he followed him. The master's footsteps led him to a place he sensed was off limits, and he hid behind Quim's legs.

Joaquim entered Dolores's room. He had been thinking about doing this for days. He wanted to examine everything, search every nook and cranny and find out what she kept there, her secrets. She shouldn't have any. She could not. Not one. A diary? He didn't think so. A letter? Surely, he would know about it. But some secret, some kind of betrayal …

There was pleasure in it, the thrill of sniffing and caressing the fabric of her clothes, fingering her necklaces and pendants and the bracelet with precious stones she got for her birthday, feeling the static sheerness of her stockings, the soft moiré of her sweaters, smelling the scent of her makeup, the fragrance of her shampoo ...

Vulgar was restless and did not wag his tail; he watched Joaquim from the door without daring to go inside. The room was his mistress's territory. When the master snuck in there at night, he covered his head with his paws, sensing a violation in the furtive entering of someone else's private space. It wasn't the same as when Victòria went in there to clean. There was something sinful about it, and a dog understands sin better than most humans.

Joaquim knew he had ample time: hair stylists are always slow and adhere to very elaborate rituals. And should Victòria and Dolores return earlier than expected, he would hear them come in. He opened drawers and felt things, he nosed around. He picked up some panties that were as soft as skin, pressed them to his face, and kissed them. A pair of stockings that were draped over a chair still held the shape of Dolores's legs. He picked them up too and peered through them: they were like a cobweb, hard and soft at the same time. They had the complexion of water. He inspected jars, tubes, bottles, makeup brushes, hairbrushes, all those mysterious little boxes on her dressing table. The clothes were neatly put away. There were a few papers lying about, but they were all essays he had assigned or poems she had copied. She had some kind of pendant made out of two glass buttons with a spider inside; what a wild little thing she still was, you only had to scratch the surface and then … a few pieces of jewellery, barrettes and hair clips, a manicure set, and that wardrobe full of dresses. In touching those objects and smelling those scents, Joaquim could feel and touch Dolores herself.

In a drawer of her nightstand Joaquim found a box, a handmade cardboard box lined with print fabric. There was money inside, quite a lot of it.

He often gave Dolores spending money, and she would use it to buy little things, she would go to the cinema or eat out or get Victòria a gift. Sometimes she asked for it, and sometimes he just gave it to her because he felt like it. 'You must never want for anything,' he would say whenever she tried to refuse his money, telling him she did not need so much. And now there it was right in front of him. All of it. He spread it out on her bed and counted it. Twenty-seven thousand, four hundred and thirty pesetas. There was no way to know for sure, but it must have been almost all the money he had ever given Dolores, a girl who rarely went out, who had all of her expenses covered. She had saved it all.

Joaquim's heart turned. Why had she kept it? Didn't she know that if she ever needed anything he would provide it? Every time Dolores had asked him for money to get an ice cream she had been lying to him: it went straight into this cardboard box lined with print fabric. Dolores was hoarding her money, stashing it away. She was saving up because she wanted to leave. A wave of pain and anger swept through Quim. How deceitful of her, how cunning; it was all a lie, it was … Putting money aside behind his back. Planning to run away. He felt like weeping. He was angry, and he was going to tell her what a backstabbing little bitch she was, what a ... He glanced at the puppy, still lingering by the door and staring at him. But what if, maybe ... ? Ah, yes, of course! She was building a nest egg for herself, to feel more independent, knowing she could buy something for herself on a whim without always having to ask. She was growing up. That was all. And besides, some people are savers, they can't help it.

He remembered the day Dolores flew into a rage, insulting the maid from the third floor and running up the stairs to give the neighbours a piece of her mind, like an army of one that fears no enemy. And he slapped her, but only to stop her rant, down deep he admired Dolores. She knew what she wanted. She was fearless and determined. And she carefully minded her money. She knew what she wanted and would never lose her way in the world. She would not be cowed. She was admirable, one of a kind!

He returned the money to its place, making sure to leave it exactly as he had found it. He was filled with gentle feelings, for he had a strong daughter, a tough, determined daughter who knew to save her money for a rainy day, who could handle anything. There was a smile on Quim's face as he left the room followed by the dog, pondering whether to open a bank account for Dolores.

The ear, round and tender. The chin firm, with a little dimple in the middle. The arch of the eyebrow perfectly formed. High breasts and low hips.

Dark desire devoid of emotion. That is what I am. A silent roar, grotesque, filled with avarice and envy. I cannot create, only contemplate.

Dolores gives a girlish laugh, then turns her back and leaves.

She is laughing at me.

When the two women returned, Quim radiated beneficence, he even patted Vulgar on the head. The dog allowed this, then ran off barking to greet Dolores. Victòria was snappy, embarrassed by her new hairstyle, which was short, curly, and auburn. Her chin trembled with indignation, though she didn't quite know what to do with her outrage. Making her pay through the nose for slapping two measly products on her! Those harpies! Crooks, they were, swindlers, scammers. Just for saying hello they expected you to fork over half of your honest earnings. She'd give them work all right, put them out in the fields to harvest esparto, or make them haul laundry, carry fruit baskets, chop firewood, pick olives ...

Quim's heart was soft; he laughed and complimented Victòria. Her rant was absurd. She wasn't the one who had paid for the hairdresser, so it made no sense for her to talk about wages and menial jobs. The hairstyle made her look plumper; it didn't suit her at all, but perhaps only a miracle would have produced better results. When she finally gathered her courage, Victòria peered at herself in the hall mirror; she delicately touched her curls, and for a moment she seemed almost enraptured as she appraised her new look. Dolores and Quim pretended not to notice but watched from the living room, exchanging impish glances.

Jon Carnisser arrived. A simple afternoon snack would not do at all: Victòria announced that she had prepared a special dinner. Cheese soufflé followed by partridge in wine sauce. As she served the meal, she absentmindedly hummed a rhythmic melody that had a Moorish cadence, and the smile on her face was like a flower, which did make her more attractive.

'You know, Jon? Dolores is like a cobweb,' Joaquim said.

'What on earth are you talking about?' Jon said. 'She's beautiful, and she's a good child.'

'That's what I mean,' Quim said. 'Have you ever looked at a cobweb closely? It's a feat of engineering, almost a miracle, lush and cool as if made of water, and at the same time very hardy.'

'And sticky enough to trap flies.'

'Imagine a newly spun web in a tree and the sun shining on it. The geometry, the perfection, the ingenuity of a structure where everything is interconnected. It's the most perfect alarm system that exists!'

'Are you saying that the girl attracts a lot of admirers?' Jon said.

'You have no sense of poetry.'

'Is there anything poetic about a fly regarded as food? What's poetic about the amount of protein a spider needs in order to survive, and the genetic code that dictates how this spider will go about obtaining it? A fly is an insect. Nothing more.'

'I'm not so sure about that; a fly's wing is a masterpiece of iridescence. Here's a question for you, Jon. Should Dolores have a bank account? Nothing excessive, just so she knows she has some money of her own.'

That night, for the first time, as he watched her sleep, he leaned down and planted a soft kiss on the girl's hair. She stirred, changing her peaceful sleeping position and revealing a neck which looked, in the dim light of the streetlamp, like frosted glass. Joaquim admired its indescribable essence, the pellucid firmness of skin that was as delicate as a sigh. Maybe a spider's web was a wonder, but Dolores's neck, and her skin, were perfection. More flawless than the nacreous skin of tender fruit, softer than the smooth surface of water, warmer than a baby's breath.

Vulgar was not waiting at the door or peering at Quim from his basket. This time he entered the room and observed the scene. He quietly drew near and put his paws on the edge of the bed next to Joaquim, and he was as motionless as an inanimate object, his breathing inaudible. Man and dog were stock-still, their eyes trained on the girl's neck, and for a moment they looked like they were bowed in prayer.

15
THE SEVENTH STEP: COMPASS (A)

AT LAST, ON A SPRING SUNDAY THAT FELT LIKE SUMMER, Dolores went up to Roses for an excursion to l'Escala in Serafí's motorboat. She had heard wonderful things about the previous outing; it had been a tremendous success. The group was the same as before: Serafí, Roser, Martí, and now Dolores. A friend of Roser's, Laura, joined them at the last minute.

It was nearly dawn by the time Dolores got home. A bleary-eyed Joaquim was waiting in his study. He said he hadn't stayed up for her but because he was reviewing a financial matter. The document on his desk lay open to the first page, and there was no sheet of paper with numbers beside it, as there always was when he was studying a business project. Exhausted but bubbling with excitement, Dolores sat down on the floor, rested her head on Quim's knees, and began to tell him everything.

The journey up to Roses in the overcrowded car had seemed long, and the conversation was superficial, the kind of talk young people indulge in. It had made Dolores miss him all the more.

'Maybe that means I'm getting older,' Dolores said.

'Or maybe you've experienced more things than the others, and it's made you more mature.'

Dolores confessed that she had a method to help her deal with boredom without seeming impatient. She fixed her gaze on a single point, just one point, and let her thoughts flow there. This softened her mood and eased her nerves. She told Quim she had concentrated on the capital *G* on the windscreen, which she thought was the initial for *Golf*, the name of the Volkswagen model that Serafí drove.

The letter g. The letter g between the two needles of a compass ...

Once they reached the coast, Dolores was as excited as the rest of them. The seaside has this effect, it calms and enlivens you at the same time. Maybe tiny sprites and fairies really did exist and lived in the salt water. Like that story you read to me, Quim ... The boat was amazing! Laura got a little seasick, but Serafí was a good captain. Roses had a pristine, white beach, and the town of l'Escala, from the water, looked like a pirate's dream. They ate their sandwiches and then they were all very thirsty. I drank so much beer I kept needing a wee. Later, they had dinner at Motel, even though Martí complained that it was a shame to do things exactly the same as the previous time; they really lacked imagination! But Serafí wanted to recreate the whole experience for Dolores.

'He did it for my sake,' she said. 'Roser was not happy. I could tell she didn't like me, but I wasn't sure what Laura thought of me, she was still sulking from being seasick. I couldn't care less.'

'What's wrong with you women, why do you dislike each other so much?' Quim stroked Dolores's messy hair. That half-undone bun, that mass of hair, reminded him of the corolla of a red flower. There was still some sand in it, and a hint of salty dampness. 'You eye one another with suspicion,' he said. 'You spy on each other and criticize each other as if you were rivals, as if each girl was, for the others, a dangerous competitor to be eliminated.'

'I don't do that!' Dolores protested.

'All of you do, and it's more frequent among pretty girls.'

'Thank goodness I'm not pretty!'

Joaquim stopped stroking her hair and pushed her away.

Dolores explained that on the way back from Roses, Serafí had insisted on going to his place for breakfast. The others were amenable, but she was not, although a cup of warm milk did sound nice.

'Why didn't you want to go?' Quim said.

Dolores was still sitting on the floor at Quim's feet, her body straight, her eyes melancholy.

'Because of you,' she said.

'Me? What nonsense. What have I got to do with it?'

'Nothing. I just missed you.'

The comment so unsettled Quim that all at once he bounded out of his armchair and almost knocked it over. He stormed out in a huff, or pretending to be in a huff, and headed to bed. There was still a lot that Dolores wanted to share with him, and she was left feeling glum, like a half-empty glass of wine after a party. Then she, too, went off to bed.

Jacint Escrivà had come to see Dolores a couple of times after sending her the flowers. He phoned repeatedly to ask her out, but Dolores never seemed to find the right moment to meet up. Maybe she was put off by the young doctor who had peered into her womb and seen how she was made inside. Over lunch one day, however, she mentioned that she was having dinner with Jacint that night, and Quim was suddenly overcome by an irrational fear that he struggled to dispel. It confused him and hampered his reasoning, pushing him into incoherence. Dolores missed him when she was in Roses, so she said, but soon enough these feelings would cease, and it would be the others she missed when she was with him. Like most fears, this one was groundless.

'Have him over for dinner,' he said.

'Why?'

'Because I say so. Period.'

Victòria, who was clearing the table, shook her head in a gesture of distilled, ancient wisdom, and mumbled that young people should mingle with other young people, it was the natural order of things; adults were a nuisance and didn't speak the same language or think alike. Above all, the old and the young didn't experience things in the same way.

Joaquim reacted to this by flying into a rage and saying horrible things that offended and humiliated Victòria. She turned around and made for the kitchen, swaying her hips as she went, proud and disdainful, with the dignity of a wounded animal that walks away without fear, without seeking revenge, and the sad pride of the blind cow in the famous poem that ambled away, languidly swishing her long tail.

And so Jacint Escrivà arrived for dinner, tongue-tied and self-conscious. A black cloud hung over Joaquim, ashamed as he was of his own insecurity and unseemly behaviour. The last thing he was prepared to admit to was fear, that was off limits, it implied weakness, and who among us can easily accept our own vulnerability?

Dinner was as slow as the ticking of the clock, gestures were awkward, conversation sluggish. The young man struggled to find something to say, and Dolores stared at her plate. Victòria burned the food, the meal she served was barely edible.

Dolores had taken up needlepoint and was working on a cushion. She had bought a frame and a canvas that already had the design printed on it. Yarns of all colours were strung out separately in a clear plastic bag. Her hair was gathered up in a crown-like bouffant, and her long house dress was sleeveless and cool. She looked like a lady from another time. She sat embroidering in the living room while Joaquim read the English and American financial press; the rustling of pages being turned sounded like birds flapping their wings.

'I'm sorry, Dolores,' he said without lowering his newspaper.

She put down the cushion and glanced at the open newspaper.

'Why do you behave like that, Quim? Why?'

Joaquim folded the paper and propped his elbows on his knees. Leaning forward, he rested his head in the palms of his hands and blurted out his apology.

'I was in a bad mood,' he said, 'but I was wrong. I make mistakes too, Dolores. I'm not perfect. The difference is I can admit it. You can go out with whoever you want, whenever you want. You know you can.'

Dolores's eyes were wide with surprise.

'But I don't give a damn about that.' She waited for Quim to scold her, but he let the vulgarity go unchallenged. 'What hurt me is the way you spoke to Victòria.'

Now it was his turn to be surprised. You could never tell how that girl would react. Who knew what went on in that head of hers?

It was midmorning, not excessively hot. The clouds had thickened, a storm was brewing, but to the east the skies were still clear. Perhaps the storm would not break until the afternoon. Loud, syncopated music was playing upstairs; the parents were probably out, and their son was taking advantage of his time alone. Or was he already married? Dolores wasn't sure. One seldom knows one's neighbours, and yet we seem to know everything about the lives and offspring of vapid celebrities, all those fake characters that populate glossy magazines and even respectable publications.

Quim announced that he was going out for a while. Dolores continued to embroider in silence. There was really no need for the cushion she was making. It had been intended for Quim, but now she had decided to give it to Victòria. After a while she got bored with the needlework and took Vulgar out for a walk; the dog sensed the oncoming storm and was restless. When they returned home, Dolores went straight to the kitchen to prepare his food. She filled his water bowl, but Vulgar wasn't thirsty. Victòria looked like she had been crying; she made little moaning sounds while she emptied the dishwasher, as if suffering from a backache, and when she bent down and stood up, she let out a profusion of sighs, a couple of ouches, and a few tired groans. She dug around in her apron pocket and pulled out a small package, unwrapped but still in the paper from the shop. She handed it to Dolores.

'Look what he gave me,' she said, 'and it's not even my Saint's Day.'

It was a bottle of a French perfume called *Poison*. The bottle itself was a work of art.

'He walked in, set it down on the table and said, here, Victòria, this is for you. It's the kind of thing that makes me turn to mush. For some people, it's seeing someone weep, others have a hard time hearing someone scream in pain. For me, what really makes me go weak in the knees is when the master feels remorse. Trust me, you won't see that very often.'

'It's his way of apologising, isn't it?' Dolores said.

'Exactly. I started crying like a baby, and now I have to pretend he didn't give me anything. I can't even thank him.'

'Why is that?'

'Ah, you silly girl. This was meant to put things behind us, don't you see? He doesn't know how to say, 'Forgive me, Victòria, I was rude and unfair.' Or do you think he would ever utter such words, a man who imagines himself so superior to everyone else? So, he leaves a gift here for me, and I know he bought it himself, he picked it out. And I can't even thank him. But I'm really touched, you see.'

Dolores didn't have the heart to tell her that Quim's gesture was meant to appease Dolores. Nor did she tell Victòria that Quim had apologized to her, and the glass bottle that held that subtle and sophisticated fragrance was actually his way of asking Dolores to forgive him. She didn't say anything, she just took Victòria's hand, her strong, red, wrinkled hand, and squeezed it.

At lunchtime, there was a piece of news that landed like a firecracker. Quim had received a letter from Jack Thurber.

'He says your father's killing was planned and carried out by a dangerous criminal organization,' Quim said. 'You were lucky he helped you get away fast. He warned me not to mention anything and not to reply to his letter. Apparently, you're still in danger. You must continue to use the name Dolores Mendoza. Maybe with time ... but right now there is a price on your head. Jack took a significant risk just by writing this letter, this crime syndicate has a global reach, they have eyes and ears everywhere.'

Dolores was not afraid; she felt safe in Barcelona with Quim. Her concern was of another kind, something deeper and harder to pin down. What frightened Dolores, and filled her with amazement, was to realize that she was forgetting her past, and that the name Thurber, and even the death of her father, was a distant echo of a time so remote she could pretend it had never existed. It was just a dream that unravelled during the day and disintegrated, evaporated, vanished a few hours after its inception. It was forgotten. And what is forgotten may as well never have been.

CHAPTER VI - TERRAE

16
THE SEVENTH STEP: COMPASS (B)

EVERY INSULT IS A PEARL/ EVERY AFFRONT A DIAMOND ... With what other senses will you have me contemplate/ this blue sky over the mountains, the vast sea, and the sun that shines on it all? His lips part from the sweet struggle/ and his eyes gleam like a dagger's blade. Happy he who lives beneath a strange sky/ and has not seen his peace disturbed/ and he who, turning a loving eye on the churning waters, has not found deception lurking there. You do not know/ what it is to watch driftwood from the wharf/ but I have seen the rain/ in buckets/drenching the boats. How many seagulls in the light of exile, how many girls clothed in nudity, how many dark glasses that avoid seeing, how many sacred elephants that read nothing. They are everywhere. Everywhere. Everywhere. They are everywhere. Like a lyre that has grown hoarse, the long hands of the wind/ played warm arpeggios through the silver rain. Men are not men if not free, men are various/ and various their languages. When I embark on a just cause/ like Tell I am unyielding and arrogant. When the war broke out/ I was fourteen years and two months old./

At first it had little effect on me. My head/ was filled with something else/ which still today I deem more important. In all of Valencia there were no lovers like us. With bouquets of light I adorn my solitude/ with bouquets of darkness I light all desire/ And I puff out my chest and dance/ though I sense the hunter's eyes watching me ...

Thus spoke our poets.

This is how things are spun together. Spindle and thread. The story is the spindle, the taut arrow where the fragile thread of words tangles.

17
THE SEVENTH STEP (THE DOOR LANDING): COMPASS (C)

VICTÒRIA WAS HEADING FROM THE DINING ROOM TO THE kitchen when she let out a moan. The tray with the not-quite-empty plates slipped from her grasp and made a loud clatter. Victòria flailed her arms like a seagull about to take flight, then dropped them, and her body slumped as if in stages, the wreck of a ship slowly sinking beneath the waters. First, in a mighty fall, she collapsed on her bottom and was left in a sitting position facing the door, her back to the table. Quim and Dolores sprang up, their bodies pitched forward, and they rushed towards that old fallen elephant. It was useless. The woman was sitting upright, her legs spread out in front of her, her jowls crumpled under the weight of her bowed, vanquished head. Her eyes were closed.

That was how Victòria died, on the floor of the dining room in her master's home, fragments of china and food scraps scattered around her.

Dolores and Joaquim crouched down, then knelt, they tried to talk to her, touched her. They shook her, and Victòria's big, defeated body fell to the side; her head bumped on the floor. They were paralysed with shock, it took them a moment to call for help, a hopeless task, for when death arrives the game is already over. Before making their way to the telephone in a daze, they noticed that as the cold hand of death was closing its grip, the woman had wet herself.

18
THE SEVENTH STEP (DESCENDING): COMPASS (D)

NO ONE ATTENDED VICTÒRIA'S FUNERAL. NOT EVEN SENYORA Rosa, who was so fond of her and sold her the juiciest, most tender meat in the market. Nor Paca, from whom she bought her eggs. Or the upstairs maid with the prominent cheekbones that Victòria thought was so nice. Nor did Teresa, who sold stockings and embroidered endlessly for other people. Nor Lluc the cobbler, who had once proposed marriage to her and suggested they share his shop's profits. Or Remigi, who worked the deli counter at the market and knew exactly how Victòria liked her grated cheese, bacon strips, and fleshy dates. Nor Gonçal the catholic schoolboy, who every year on March 13 sold her a votive candle to light in memory of her husband. Not the greengrocer, the fishmonger, or Roser, who owned the haberdashery that Victòria patronized. Quimeta, her old neighbour from the time when Victòria was married, who used to look after her son, was not in attendance either, for she had died ten years before. Maybe even twenty.

It was a brilliant summer day, a cheerful sun fell on the niches. Joaquim and Dolores had been alone at Sancho de

Ávila funeral parlour, and now they were alone at the cemetery. They avoided each other's gaze and said nothing. They had a lump in their throats, the heavy sadness of their stunned grief. A nameless priest uttered a few words and then, slap, slap, slap, the workers closed up the niche with clumps of plaster. Dolores took Quim's hand, which hung limp like the sleeve of an empty coat on a hanger. He made no effort to hold hers. Neither of them wept. Slap, slap, slap went the plaster. The spatula the workers used to smooth it over left circular tracks. It was grey, but as the sun beat down on it, the plaster slowly turned white.

Their hands were still joined when they turned around and headed toward the gates of Montjuïc Cemetery. On the way down they met Ramon, the bread boy, who was holding a bouquet of golden flowers and looking pale. He glanced at them but didn't say anything, and together the three of them proceeded down the hill in silence. Ramon forgot to leave the flowers by Victòria's niche. There was almost no traffic at that hot hour of the day and the click-clacking of three pairs of shoes resounded on the pavement.

PART THREE
BLACK

CHAPTER VII – RECTIFICANDO

19
THE SEVENTH STEP (DESCENDING): COMPASS (E)

THEY SAT SILENTLY FOR HOURS. THE FLAT SEEMED APPALLINGLY empty. Joaquim refused to share his thoughts, as if ashamed of his grief, and when he finally spoke, he clicked his tongue and said: 'At the end of the day, she was just a maid, the world is full of them.' But he looked like a man who had lost his way in a strange land. Vulgar whimpered and clung to Dolores, as if he had seen Victòria's shadow and was afraid.

Dolores asked that they not hire a new maid; it would be an insult for someone to take possession of Victòria's kitchen, her bedroom, what had been her domain. 'Nonsense,' Joaquim declared. So Dolores's second request was to run the home herself. 'As you wish,' Joaquim said. 'We'll find someone to help out, but I think you're being overly sentimental about this; whoever we hire, whether it's a maid or some other kind of help, they will surely need to go in the kitchen at some point, no? And I won't have you cleaning or cooking, so get that out of your head.' She begged Quim to let her take full charge of things, at least until they could find hired help. The idea pleased her. She hadn't realized he was snobbish enough to forbid her to work. But Quim was adamant, and nothing could be done. He was the one who swept the floor that first day. All Dolores was allowed to do was prepare some cold sandwiches for them.

The time eventually came when they had to enter the hallowed ground of Victòria's bedroom. Neither of them had ever set foot in there before. Dolores had come close to it the day she arrived, but even then, she had only stood at the threshold. The woman's presence could still be felt, the room had her smell, the large dresses that hung in the closet still held her shape, and so many of her personal belongings were scattered about that their hearts sank, and they tiptoed out of the room, as if afraid of scaring a sleeping ghost.

Quim sat down and scratched his chin. As people with money are wont to do when faced with a disagreeable task, he wondered who could clear out the room for them. Someone with no interest in the matter other than earning a bit of money. Someone whose hands wouldn't tremble. Neither of them had said a word since they had crept out of that bedroom filled with memories of Victòria. Now they sat staring into mid-air. When Dolores spoke, it was as if they had been in the middle of a conversation and words, not hazy thoughts, had filled their lassitude. 'I don't think she had any family. But Ramon, maybe he could ...' Joaquim did not reply.

Dolores phoned the bakery. Both she and Quim were surprised to learn that Ramon no longer worked there; he had left months before. He did have a home number that they could give her. They had been pleased with Ramon; he had even helped them find someone to replace him, but truth be told, the new guy wasn't on top of things yet. What could they do? Boys become men and want men's wages; that's how things go.

Ramon wasn't there when Dolores called his home. The woman who answered the phone said she was his mother and asked Dolores how she was doing. She remembered her from when she had gone to see Ramon after poor little Tom was crushed by the lorry. Dolores could not remember meeting Ramon's mother and could not have described what she looked like. If an image of the woman had reached Dolores's retina, it had never crossed the barrier of memory, but faded silently from her mind, like cigarette smoke at an open window.

The woman promised to pass on the message and told Dolores not to fret; her Ramon was very reliable, unlike most boys today, who were running wild; he'd never caused her to lose any sleep, how very fortunate, considering how things were going nowadays ... The same grievances, voiced by each new generation since time immemorial. The lost golden years. The innocence locked away at the bottom of the deepest drawer, the key tossed into the sea, lost and gone for ever. The glorious past. Oh, the past. So remote now. How sad that it was over!

The past does not exist, and we don't seem to realize it.

They found some steaks in the freezer and defrosted them in a frying pan because neither of them knew how the microwave worked, and where had the instructions manual gone? There was a knock on the door. Joaquim went to answer it and came back to the kitchen with Ramon. He seemed taller now, more manly, or could it be that needing him made him suddenly appear older in their eyes? He agreed to stay for dinner, but only if they let him do the cooking; he knew how to work the microwave, and frying steaks that were still half frozen was not a good idea. Ramon had other skills too, such as running the washing machine and the dishwasher, which he explained to them very slowly, as if they were both thick.

They had supper in the kitchen. Ramon even found some *escalivada* in the back of the freezer. Quim told Dolores that she might have spent hours helping Victòria, but Ramon knew his way around the kitchen better than she did ... there are those of us who pay attention, and those who simply follow instructions and never know the why of things. 'I tested this out once, and it never fails,' he said. 'Whenever I came across a group of workers digging a ditch in the street, I asked them what the ditch was for. There were three kinds of answers. I say *ditch*, but I might as well be saying *surgical operation* or *accounting method*. It's the same everywhere. There's the person who says the ditch is to lay a cable because the traffic light is out of order and needs fixing; there's the one who says it's meant for an electrical wire but doesn't know what role the wire plays or the purpose of any of it. And then there is the one who shrugs his shoulders and says he doesn't know, he was told to dig and that's what he's doing.'

Joaquim spoke in a sad voice, not meaning to challenge Dolores or offend her, but as if describing a spell of bad luck that was not worth struggling against because it would be a waste of time. Ramon and Dolores didn't say anything, they ate in silence.

Joaquim and Dolores finally told Ramon that they needed

to clean out Victòria's room. He nodded, as if he understood it was too delicate a task for them. 'The best thing would be to phone Caritas or one of those charities that collects secondhand clothes,' he said. 'They'll clear it out in no time, and if they have any objections, I'm sure the problem can be solved with a tip. I'll supervise if you want, so they won't steal anything.' It sounded like a good idea, but it seemed odd to give things away to charity and at the same time worry about being robbed. It was a notion that Victòria herself might have entertained.

In a slow drawl that made it seem as if the question was more important than the answer, Quim asked Ramon why he had gone to the cemetery.

'I couldn't get off work in time to make it to the funeral home,' Ramon said. 'I felt terrible about it.' He explained that it was Victòria who had found him the job at the injection moulding factory; she knew the person in charge and had recommended him. Senyor Manuel, the manager, said he preferred training Ramon to hiring a more experienced candidate because he had been sent by Victòria. He had learnt quickly. 'Although I did mess up my first day on the job,' Ramon said, 'and I thought I was going to be sacked.' He had already been at the factory for six months and was earning a good salary, not the pittance he used to make at the bakery, which belonged to the Stingy Guild and exploited him to boot; he had been hired as an errand boy, but he was always being asked to cart sacks and load and empty the ovens, which wasn't his responsibility. He was happy at his new job; he knew that Senyor Manuel would be retiring soon and wanted to recommend Ramon for the manager position, even though other workers had been there longer than he had. 'That's still a year away,' he said, 'and by then I'll know the ropes better than anyone else.'

Dolores suddenly felt that hers was an empty life; all those plans and projects, all that striving, and the joy of moving up in life and making more money, those things were beyond her reach. She felt a bitter pang of envy, just a trace, tiny and round like a grain of millet.

'This Senyor Manuel, how did he know Victòria?' she asked. 'She didn't have many friends or acquaintances as far as I know; she never really did much and she went out very little. Mostly to do the shopping, but that's about it.'

'I think Senyor Manuel had been a friend of her husband's when they were young,' Ramon said. 'He and his wife are from Andalucia, but they speak better Catalan than you and me. Victòria had been to their place many times, they used to hold clandestine meetings or something political like that. No matter how many times I asked, Victòria refused to tell me how her husband died. I think it must have had to do with the repression during the Franco dictatorship. Senyor Manuel asked me to take some flowers to the funeral parlour for him, but then the factory owner showed up and I couldn't just absent myself and leave Senyor Manuel holding the bag. I told myself, well, go to the cemetery then, and say goodbye to Victòria.'

Ramon found some boys from a youth organization that delivered aid to the developing world, mostly students and conscientious objectors doing community services. In half an hour they had all of Victòria's belongings loaded into a van, everything but her gold-plated chain with the pendant of the Virgin Mary. They were decent young men, incapable of pocketing a piece of jewellery, even one as insignificant as that. When they showed Dolores the pendant, her first impulse was to give it away, but then she held out her hand and took it, and she fastened it around her neck. The medallion felt cold against her skin, but it warmed up immediately. They should have put it on Victòria when she died.

Ramon also brought in someone to help around the flat, a young woman, short and spirited, with an easy laugh, who did the work quickly so she could leave early. No one supervised Emília, but she was reliable and ran the home with a swift, efficient hand. Occasionally, she did the shopping, but she wasn't a great cook, so Quim gave Dolores permission to prepare lunch and dinner. 'We'll eat out most days, fewer headaches that way. You can order the groceries over the phone, Dolores, and if that turns out to be more expensive and not as good, so be it,' he said. 'I do not want to see you dragging a shopping trolley and queuing at the fish monger or the meat stall. We'll find someone else for that, another woman, some other day. When we are ready. And eventually we'll get Victòria out of our heads, out of our home, but right now she's still everywhere, you can almost hear her voice, her footsteps, her constant whingeing, and you feel like a stranger in your own kitchen.'

Victòria's bedroom was empty. The painters had come and transformed the place from top to bottom. The old scent of her room was washed away. 'Should we set up a workspace for you in here?' Quim said. 'Your bedroom is looking a bit cluttered with the computer and everything; we can put up some shelves, get a desk for your computer and another one for studying. You haven't applied yourself in ages, Senyoreta, this won't do at all!'

Quim and Dolores went shopping and bought some Japanese blinds, an Italian floor lamp, and a desk that came with a filing cabinet and a drawer that—oh!—you could lock with a key. But the best was the recliner that Quim chose for her, which was just like his but smaller. She would spend hours sitting in it, playing like a child. Entering Victòria's room, now that it had been painted and redecorated and newly transformed into a home office, was not scary any more.

Dolores was rather a good cook, as it turned out. Going out for meals was a bit of a hassle, so they almost always had lunch at home. By now, the kitchen held no more secrets for her, and sometimes she even kicked Quim out, as if she were the mistress of the home. Or the maid.

Summer was at its peak; the air conditioning was on all day. Dolores bought geraniums and carnations. Little by little, she learned to manage the housemaid. She didn't go out much, only to walk Vulgar, do the shopping with Quim, or dine at a restaurant together. On hot afternoons, Dolores donned a pair of shorts and a shabby old T-shirt and shut herself in *her* study. She turned off the air conditioning: she didn't like it. Quim would put his eye to the keyhole and see her in there reading books, looking serious and focused. Seeing her like that made his heart sing

20
THE SIXTH STEP (DESCENDING): PLUMB LINE (A)

SERAFÍ RENOM HAD COME TO COLLECT DOLORES, AND THERE was no getting out of it: he was taking her out to dinner and a show. He was good-looking, despite the little smirk he often had on his face, a quirk seen in people who are proud but insecure. He had a golden tan, dressed well, and looked people in the eye with a friendly, velvety gaze that made them feel safe and heard.

The two of them had dinner at a posh restaurant. Serafí did all the talking at first; he told Dolores that his father was unbearable, and there were no honest bankers. He wanted more out of life, but he didn't know what exactly. He looked like a child when he said this, it inspired tenderness, but the glint in his eyes revealed that passing himself off as a hapless young man was just a ploy to get under people's skin.

But then Dolores took over the conversation, and since she hardly ever talked to anyone, she found that she had a lot to say. Serafí's short, friendly questions put her at ease and encouraged her to speak at length. She told him everything, meaning the version of events she and Quim had agreed on:

after her parents died Uncle Quim adopted her, and now she was starting to forget her old life; it was almost as if it had never happened, and she had dreamed up the whole thing rather than lived it.

Serafí was shocked to learn about her present circumstances. 'You're living like a prisoner,' he told her. 'Why are you afraid of him?' Dolores denied this so adamantly, so vehemently, that it was plain that she was indeed afraid of Quim. How she wished Victòria were there! 'You need to look out for your own interests,' Serafí said. 'The people we lose seem more important than they ever were in life, until one day we forget about them completely. I wouldn't care at all if my father died.'

The truth was she didn't know what she wanted either. Her days slipped by, and things were good enough. But now that Victòria was gone, Dolores felt a new listlessness.

'You're not underage any more,' Serafí said.

Dolores felt looked after by Quim. He was a good father and would do anything for her; he bought her lots of things and didn't let her do any housework.

'Your life is in your hands.'

But life had been sucked out of her; she used to be so active, but now there was an emptiness inside her.

'You have rights, you know?' Serafí insisted. 'He adopted you, so you have full legal rights. Financially, I mean.'

If only she had a project, a purpose, an idea. Something to occupy her time. A profession. An obligation.

'And you should be financially independent; that's more important than anything else, especially if you have some money of your own.'

Maybe it was fear, Dolores thought, or perhaps gratitude, or the fact that she had agreed to be tutored by Quim, for after all she had been old enough to reject certain things. She did not wish to cause him pain.

'Tomorrow,' Serafí said, 'you just leave the flat without telling him anything, you don't owe him an explanation. I won't come and get you. You come to me. When you're dressed, you just say, I'm going out now. And if he asks where to, tell him you're going for a walk and you'll be back later.'

Quim picked up the dog and plopped him on his lap. Sitting in the rocking chair that Dolores usually occupied, he stroked the animal, then lifted him up. They looked into each other's eyes. Vulgar's soft gaze was full of affection. Quim felt ill. 'I'm just like you, Vulgar,' he told the dog. 'We're the same, you and I, we don't think much, which is only natural for you because you're a dog. But what am I?'

I'm a dog. I rear my tragic head and howl in anguish. My long, chilling yowls slice through layers of misery and hit the target of grief. I howl frightfully, alone. I howl like a dog because that is what I am, a dog. I'm howling because you are beautiful, Dolores, and you are slipping through my fingers.

'Maybe I'm going crazy, Vulgar, if a madman can ever know that he is mad. I must speak with Jon; he's a lawyer and will know what to do, though he already warned me that it's not possible to renounce paternity after adoption.'

Vulgar licked his face, and Quim noticed that his wet tongue was becoming a little scratchy. Let's say he did something to the dog. Dolores would do anything to keep it from happening again. He could get her to do whatever he wanted. Anything at all. He would have to overcome his disgust at the idea of hurting the animal. But why would that give him pause? It was just a silly dog. It was a fleeting thought, like the gleam of a camera flash. Now that Victòria was gone nobody was watching him. No witnesses. If he wanted to, or could, or even knew how …

When Dolores got home, Joaquim was in his room with the lights off but still awake, his head filled with worry. She stood in the middle of the living room for a moment, as if listening. Quim held his breath. It was late, and quite stuffy. Maybe if he had waited up for her, she would have sat on the floor and rested her head on his knees, and told him what she had been up to, where she had gone. Maybe she would have said that she had missed him.

The following day Dolores wandered aimlessly about the flat, lost in reverie. Quim took this as a bad omen. She barely said a word, and the lunch she prepared for them was bland. Vulgar begged to be walked but she didn't even look at him. Quim took pity on the dog, he fed him and gave him a few clumsy pats. In the afternoon Dolores shut herself in her bedroom rather than her study, and she stayed there for hours. Who knew what she was doing? Quim paced up and down like a prisoner. Around seven o'clock, when the sun had started to ease off and slowly creep westward, Dolores reappeared, all dressed up, and made for the door. 'Adéu, Quim. I'm going out,' she said as she walked past him. Before he could react, the door slammed shut. Quim stood there with his mouth open and his hands behind his back, stunned and turtle-faced, staring at the door. Then he collapsed into a chair and wept; long threads of snot dripped onto his knees. He felt an upwelling of rage and clenched his fists.

Serafí's home wasn't far but Dolores took a taxi, walking there would have been too much of an effort. The streets were nearly empty. She should have her own car, she thought, and was saddened to realize that she was faced with a choice: stand up for herself and make a bid for freedom or continue to beg for gifts. She couldn't have it both ways. The logic of it was unimpeachable.

The Renoms were away for the summer, the father came and went from l'Escala, but today was Friday and Serafí was alone in the apartment. This was news to Dolores. Serafí answered the door in a bathing suit; he had been on the terrace soaking up the enfeebled and dusty Barcelona sun. Dolores lived a sheltered life and was not always familiar with social norms and standards of behaviour. 'So, you're on your own?' she asked him. Serafí told her that the rest of the family were away. 'Great, no?' He said he had stayed in town to run a few errands, and also to see her, since they'd agreed to meet up. 'I didn't really think you'd come; that's why I'm not properly dressed.'

But the feeling of trust they had enjoyed the previous night at the restaurant was gone. Dolores wasn't happy at all. She couldn't find the words to convey to Serafí just how difficult it had been for her to break her habit of asking for permission to go out or even of staying at home. In her white blouse and Bermuda shorts, Dolores looked svelte, her hair down to her shoulders, her temples glistening with sweat.

Serafí led her into the air-conditioned living room and prepared an exotic, refreshing drink that tasted both sweet and bitter. He played some music, a languid, rhythmic tune that reminded Dolores of an animal lying in the shade. He twirled her around, placed the flat of his hand on her back and put his cheek to hers, breathing gently in her ear without speaking. He ran his hand up and down her spine and squeezed her fingers. Dolores's eyes closed. The fragrant sweat of Serafí's body filled her with desire; she caressed his skin and listened to the beating of his heart.

The music was still playing when they lay down on his bed. He made love to her slowly, with the skill of a man who knew how to please. She allowed him to enter her and was surprised to feel such pleasure, for she had thought she would never enjoy sex. Her own courage was the best aphrodisiac. Afterwards, they showered together and had a bite to eat in the glistening kitchen. She felt strange, as if dissociated from her own body, but she laughed at the boy's jokes. In the bathroom again, this time alone, she touched her breasts, her thighs, her wet sex, not quite believing it was her own body she was feeling. She banished any hint of worry from her mind. But then she glanced at her watch. Midnight. Quim would be worried.

Like the previous night, the flat was dark and quiet. Like the previous night, Dolores stopped for a moment and listened for any sounds coming from Quim's bedroom. Like the night before, Quim held his breath and waited, and after the door to Dolores's room had been closed for a long time, he got up, as always, and slowly tiptoed into her room to watch her sleeping. Dolores's face was buried in her pillow. All he could see was a mass of hair that cascaded down to her nape in two separate bunches. He was drawn like a magnet to the back of that neck, which flaunted itself between the parted hair like the open sex of a woman.

Then he noticed something. At first, he didn't know what it was, he couldn't put his finger on the cause of his anguish. He tried to reason with himself. It's the scent, he finally decided. Dolores didn't have her usual soapy smell. He picked up her clothes and sniffed them. Her panties held the smell, the unmistakable traces, of sex. Still holding her clothes in his hands, pale as death, Quim looked at Dolores with murderous jealousy.

The next day, Dolores announced that she was going out, but when she tried to open the front door, it was locked. She searched for the key; it wasn't there, nor could she find it anywhere else in the apartment.

Dolores entered Joaquim's study, where he was working, and protested.

'You will go out when I say you can,' he told her. 'You will do as I want. Now, get out. I've work to do.'

'I'm an adult now!' Dolores said.

'You are whatever age I say you are. Out!'

Dolores was furious. She had been thinking about going out and wondering whether that was what she really wanted to do. A repeat of yesterday's game didn't hold much appeal, and she wasn't sure that seeing Serafí was a good idea, it just wouldn't be the same. But being locked up was infuriating.

The door onto the covered balcony off the kitchen was also locked. She closed all the other doors, turned up the volume on the television, wrapped a towel around the end of the broomstick and charged at the glass. It didn't break. She tried again and again, sweating profusely, stubborn in her fury. She opened the tool cabinet and grabbed a heavy hammer. The glass crumbled like flour, it shattered like a toxic storm, covering her with bits of glass from head to toe. Somehow, she was not hurt.

It was not difficult to get to the ground level from the back balcony. All it took was one good jump. The soft soil of the garden cushioned her landing. Dolores straightened up, tired, hot, and furious, her hands swollen. She walked away without stopping to think about how she would get back inside. For now, she was winning.

No one answered the door at Serafí's apartment. They had not agreed to meet up, that was true, but it would be strange for him to leave without saying anything. What happened yesterday was important. Right?

She strolled around, went into a café and ordered a slushy, and window-shopped. The streets were semi deserted. Dolores was getting tired, and she started dragging her feet, not really knowing which direction to take. Around evening time, she stopped by Serafí's place again; he must have been out earlier, he would never leave for l'Escala like that, without saying anything ...

The doorbell rang in an empty flat.

Night fell. Dolores gave up and went home. Maybe Quim wouldn't open the door. Maybe no one wanted her. Maybe she had not behaved very well. But Quim had only intended to punish her, he wouldn't abandon her. She remembered Thurber's letter saying that a criminal organization was searching the world for her and for a moment she panicked.

She stood at the front door for nearly twenty minutes, trying to muster the courage to ring the doorbell. Climbing up to the kitchen gallery was much harder than jumping down.

Quim had done nothing about the broken door, leaving the place vulnerable to thieves. There was glass everywhere. It ripped her clothes and cut her hands, but Dolores hoisted herself up, grabbed the balcony railing and clambered over it. She lay down on the floor, panting from the enormous effort. The flat was quiet. Maybe no one was there. But that wasn't possible. Where could Quim have gone? Where would he go without her?

Gathering her courage, Dolores slowly opened the door to Quim's bedroom and saw, in the dim light, his undisturbed bed. She walked around. He wasn't there. Dolores felt guilty. She was trapped in a maze, wandering around aimlessly, unable to find her way out. Exhausted, she decided to go to bed. She didn't turn on the light in her room. Who knew what tomorrow might bring? Perhaps if she apologized to him ...

Her scream shot through the dark like a paper arrow in a sea of fog. Dolores shrieked until she was almost choking, her eyes small with terror. She collapsed and felt as if she was vomiting fire. Her face was flushed, her roiling blood rushed up her neck. Vulgar's lifeless body lay on the bed, his head slumped on her pillow, a knife still stuck in his neck. The bed was soaked with blood. Dolores fainted.

21
THE SIXTH STEP (DESCENDING): PLUMB LINE (B)

SEVEN DAYS PASSED, EACH OF THEM TWENTY-FOUR LONG hours. The front door was still locked, and Joaquim was gone. Dolores thought she might be going mad. She couldn't leave and she couldn't have anyone over. She could call the fire brigade, but what would she tell them? How would she explain the situation she was in? She paced up and down for hours, half undressed and barefoot, her hair all tangled. She wept and wept. She slept on the leather sofa in the living room and woke up drenched in sweat. She cried some more, walked around the flat, despaired. She weathered every bad feeling: rage, anger, hatred, helplessness, humiliation ... she suffered through it all, and little by little she felt herself going insane.

After two days without food, a furious hunger gnawed at her. There wasn't much in the refrigerator, and what she found she ingested raw. She drained the liquor cabinet. She wept wildly, her hair a mess, her feet bare. Vulgar's body gave off a terrible stench.

On the fourth day she came to her senses. She swept up the broken glass and wrapped the dog in the blood-stained bedspread, feeling her stomach turn. She avoided looking at Vulgar. Using a rope, she devised a way to lower his body down to the garden. Fortunately, it was mid-August, and all the neighbours were away. Then she took a shovel and jumped down, recalling how Victòria had handled things the day Dolores had killed the cat. If Victòria had been there, Quim would never have dared to hurt her dog.

She buried Vulgar deep in the ground at the other end of the garden, steering well clear of the feline remains of that disgusting Foof. She brought down the potted carnation to mark his grave. Then she clambered back up to the flat and decided to wash, prepare a proper meal, and clean the place. She did it all in a frenzy, trying to quiet her thoughts, for she sensed the threat of madness beating in her head, taunting her, watching her, waiting for her to let down her guard to take full possession of her.

She boarded up the broken door with cardboard. She fried some eggs and prepared instant soup from a packet. Now she was showered, her hair combed, and the flat smelled good after spraying air freshener. Dolores considered the situation. She could not open the front door, so she could not order groceries over the phone from the one supermarket that was still open in August. Even if she found someone to fix the broken glass, there was no way to let the person in. She had some money saved, but she couldn't find the key to the apartment, and the door had been dead bolted on purpose to deter burglars.

The most challenging task was the bed. She threw the sheets in the rubbish bin, which was already overflowing. She scrubbed the mattress with soap and hot water and left it in a sunny spot to dry; she would have to turn it over later to avoid any lingering dampness and the horror of that faded stain. Using a rope, she lowered the binbags to the garden. She drank a lot of milk, of that there was plenty. She prepared another meal, she boiled rice and roasted potatoes in the oven. She drank all the wine she could find, and the whisky, and the gin. Joaquim did not allow her to have any alcohol, apart from a sip of wine with her meals. Now she drank, not to indulge but to survive.

In all this time the phone had rung three times, but she did not answer. She wondered where Emília, the new maid, could be, and decided that before doing his dark deed Joaquim had told her not to come. What if he never returned? She could always call the fire department, but appearing in the news might spell disaster, the criminal gang that was after her was savvy and powerful. She repressed a twinge of despair and focused on organizing her day. Her foremost concern was the lack of food. There was a knock at the door. Dolores looked through the peephole and spied the postman. She ignored him. Another day, a man stood on the other side of the door shouting that he was from the gas company. Dolores remained silent. How many more days could she hold out?

On the seventh day, she was cleaning the bathroom when she heard the door, then footsteps. Quim's familiar footsteps. Bent over the bathtub with her back to the door, she stopped scrubbing and went stiff. The feelings that had been tormenting her were suddenly subdued, dull, painful rumblings drained of their power. Quim was standing at the bathroom door. Dolores continued scrubbing, as if she were deaf. 'You know I don't like you doing this kind of work,' he said. Then he turned around and left. That was all Quim said: for her not to clean. Maybe he really was insane. Not maybe, he most certainly was. Dolores was confused, she didn't know what to do or what to say. A knock at the front door. Then Dolores heard the familiar sound of the grocery store's delivery guy unloading parcels in the kitchen. She straightened up and stopped scrubbing. She went into the kitchen and started putting away the groceries without a word. It was mid-morning, but she immediately started cooking. Joaquim didn't say anything either, he let her get on with her chores. She ate in the kitchen, alone, her hunger pinching the walls of her stomach like crab claws. She ate until she was exhausted. There was another knock on the front door: a repairman greeted her and set about replacing the broken glass in the door to the back gallery. After he finished, Dolores glanced down at the garden and saw that the pile of binbags was gone. Quim must have thrown them in the dumpster. She heard him calling her from his study.

He was sitting behind his desk, his brow deeply furrowed.

'I'm sorry you went hungry,' he said. 'I didn't think about that.'

Dolores was stunned, her hands cold, a fiery look in her eyes.

'But I must say I'm pleased,' Quim told her. 'Not only did you manage on your own, but you kept the place neat and tidy. You have some good qualities, Dolores.'

Dolores exploded with loud insults, calling him a murderer, an evil person. She spat on him; a bit glob of saliva landed on his cheek. Joaquim rose from his chair, circled the desk, and grabbed Dolores by the wrists.

'Calm down and start acting civilised, or I will strike you, Dolores.'

'Civilised?' She was on the verge of losing control. 'What is civilised about killing a poor dog? You tell me!'

'I didn't kill him, Dolores. You did.'

She gasped.

Little by little, Joaquim managed to calm her down. He knew her well, he said, and he had always sensed that old, despicable vices were at the core of who she was. He had been right all along.

'You fed me that story about a rape,' he said. 'You who are so wild, raped by someone like Jack Thurber? Ha! That's when I knew. As soon as you had the chance, you rolled in the hay with the first man that came along. And here I have tried to look after you. I've lost sleep over you. It's your nature, Dolores! So, I had to punish you. I am responsible for you. It pains me, but I took on this responsibility and I cannot go back on it. I had to punish you. Can't you see?'

Dolores didn't know how to respond; his words cut like a knife, and she was starting to feel guilty. In his presence, her judgement turned to mush.

'Can't you understand?' Quim said. 'It had to be something you would never forget. It broke my heart, the poor dog, you know how I loved him. But I had no choice.'

I only meant to hurt him, so you'd feel sorry and repent. I needed him alive so I could use him on other occasions. I was holding him down, and he was half asleep. I had injected him with a sedative to keep his suffering to a minimum. But then he jerked his head. That silly dog stabbed himself. All I was after was a little neck wound, a visible wound to make you feel pity. I never intended to kill him! This is the truth, Dolores. If only I could tell you and you could understand!

'So don't accuse me of something you brought on yourself,' Joaquim told Dolores. 'You went to bed with a man. And I had to punish you for it.'

Strangely enough, Dolores settled down and started nodding. She leaned against his chest. Joaquim held her gently and spoke to her in a sweet voice, repeating that he had done it for her, it was the only way to tame her.

When at last she was calm and docile, he pushed her away and removed something from his pocket. He held up a bunch of keys. 'You're not a prisoner,' he said. 'If you want to go out, you just need to ask permission and tell me where you're going. That's all. It's not very much to ask. Ah, and never lie to me, Dolores. Otherwise, I will have to punish you again.'

She had not cried when he said demeaning things to her, but now she felt like weeping. Through the fog that enveloped her sanity she sensed that she was utterly lost and in the hands of a madman. Her will was slowly being eroded. She had not behaved well, on that they both agreed.

'I have a present for you,' Joaquim told her. 'Come with me.' He led her down the stairs, holding her by the arm when her step faltered. A brand-new car was parked in front of the building, gleaming white. He dangled another set of keys in front of her. 'It's all yours,' he said. 'Here, the keys. Tomorrow, I'll start teaching you how to drive. See? You can go wherever you want and do whatever you wish. You just need to get my permission.' He lifted her chin, forcing her to look at him. 'I'm sorry,' she whispered, so faintly he could barely hear it, and it was the look she gave him more than her words that allowed him to understand what she was saying. They got in the car. Dolores felt a jolt of joy. It was new, with lovely interiors, and it was her very own. She threw her arms around Quim's neck and gave him a big *gràcies* as splendid as the morning sun.

The driving lessons began the very next day, as promised. It was the perfect time for it because there was little traffic in the summer months. Besides, Dolores already had some driving experience. Nobody mentioned the dog, though Quim spotted the carnation in the communal garden and immediately knew what it meant.

Their usual routines resumed, and Dolores and Quim seemed to get along as well as they had before. Dolores understood the rules: she had to obey him. What if she ran away? No, those men would track her down. She could have it all, anything she wanted, but she must follow the rules, and no sleeping around ever again. What if he was right? Maybe she deserved what had happened. But she was free. All she had to do was ask. She had a car, a bank account, even some savings. To get whatever she wanted, all she had to do was ask. So long as she did exactly what he told her. That was all. What kind of life would that be? A good enough life. It had a lot of advantages.

'We'll drive up to Blanes tomorrow,' Quim said. 'I know how much you liked it there. We can spend a few days at the seaside. There's a hotel where they know who I am, and even if it's high season they won't turn us away. Are you all sorted for beachwear?'

What if Quim really was crazy? She would have to play along. She'd agree to everything, she'd obey. She would need to trick him, but she would have to plan it well and be cleverer than he was.

'Do you really want us to go to the beach?' she said. 'Won't it be too crowded? Maybe we could just stay here.'

Quim's face lit up. He preferred that too.

'You know what I'd like?' Dolores said.

'What?' He seemed anxious to please her.

'I want to show Ramon the car, and maybe he can give me driving lessons. Also give me driving lessons, I mean.'

'It's done.'

Quim put his arm around Dolores's shoulders, as if protecting her. He could trust Ramon. And if he caused any trouble, he would swat him away like a fly.

CHAPTER VIII – INVENIES

22
THE FIFTH STEP (DESCENDING): LEVEL (A)

HAPPY TIMES FOLLOWED, FOR SUCH IS THE HUMAN ABILITY to adapt to circumstances, to root oneself in the earth and push through the highs and lows of life, as hard as that may be, to sing alone without thinking about it when the storm rages and surviving is a struggle.

Dolores and Joaquim entered a period of harmony that felt as immutable as the fecundity of the earth and the flow of a high mountain spring. A mild autumn came, followed by a late winter of dry cold and deep blue, cloudless skies. Victòria had ceased to exist, and Vulgar was just the hint of a frozen smile that lingers on one's lips on a long, drawn-out evening.

They no longer had Emília, the short, jovial cleaning woman who shaved a few minutes off the hours that she was paid. Joaquim hired a cleaning company run by men who worked with detached and expeditious efficiency. Generally, two of them came to the flat, and they would ask Quim and Dolores to either leave or stay out of the way. They behaved like contractors commandeering the home for a few hours and left everything so aseptically clean and disinfected that the entire place seemed to have been boiled and converted into a modern hospital ward. Once a week was more than enough. If something needed to be repaired, the same company provided a painter, a handyman, a plumber. Everything ran smoothly.

Quim and Dolores shopped at their usual grocery store, phoning in their order, which was then delivered by a young man who always made recommendations. 'We've just received some lamb,' he'd say, 'straight from Girona, and it's tender as butter, trust me on this. And we have new potatoes. The oranges are a bit bitter, but the grapes are sweet as honey; you must try them. Perhaps you'd like some real foie gras? A shipment has just arrived from France. Not cheap, but you won't find anything like it in all of Barcelona.' The delivery man was also one of the owners, and he was a good salesman.

Quim suggested to Dolores that they cook together; he said it was an art form, like painting, and it took some effort. Not everyone was good at it. He bought some cookery books and the two of them stood at the kitchen table like soldiers, in dazzling white aprons and even chef's hats, the ingredients lined up in front of them. They would follow the recipes until they were confident enough to improvise. Dolores's previous knowledge was shelved, this was about creating a daily work of art, not your average home-cooked meal that anyone who put his mind to it could prepare.

It was great fun. They rose at about ten in the morning and had breakfast together while planning their meal. At one o'clock, operation lunch began. They took it very seriously, and they had a lot of fun. If they ever spoiled a dish, the culprit would not admit defeat but rather argue that the flavour was unique even if it took getting used to, only a discerning palate would appreciate its exquisite taste. Quim and Dolores engaged in a friendly culinary rivalry. They hardly ever dined out. Their evening meals were simple fare, often leftovers from lunch, for they always miscalculated and made more than two servings; the only drawback was having to eat the same thing again. They pictured themselves delivering their leftovers to the pompous notary on the second floor or those lunatics on the third floor. *We thought you might like to try some of this; it's all homemade.* They would imagine their neighbours' awkward reaction and burst out laughing.

They resumed hosting dinner parties at home. Serafí Renom declined their first invitation, but Joaquim insisted; he wanted to prove to Dolores that he had put his old animosity behind him. Nevertheless, when Serafí finally did show up, Joaquim watched him closely. His presence intimidated Dolores; the fact that he had never contacted her again made her feel ashamed and confused, but she had mastered the subtle art of putting on a brave face in the presence of those you dislike. When Serafí left, she and Quim sighed with relief, each for their own reasons. Serafí never suspected that he was the cause of unspoken tension between Quim and Dolores; he would have sworn that Dolores had put their affair behind her, just as he had, and that Joaquim never knew anything about it.

Jacint Escrivà, the serious young doctor who was the son of a doctor, also started coming round, having long since gotten over the tense dinner that he and Dolores had shared the previous year. He sneaked glances at her, and she ignored him, but Quim noticed and took pleasure in provoking him, relishing the moment, feeling superior.

Dolores had become a rather good driver, especially since Ramon had started coming over to give her driving lessons. He had bought a small van and boasted about being better than a taxi driver at navigating the streets of Barcelona. Dolores's car took them on a thousand outings, but only on weekends, during the week Ramon was either too busy or too tired. If they ever went to the cinema, or to that snazzy nightclub that had recently opened at the top of Carrer Muntaner, they asked Joaquim to join them, but he always declined. 'You young people run along and stay out of my hair,' he'd say.

He always allowed Dolores to go out. Always. But having his permission was essential. More than brushing her teeth in the morning or undressing for bed at night. More than paying the bills or putting on her coat before leaving the flat. More than turning on the heat, doing laundry, watering the plants. It was more important than breathing. And as is usually the case with habits, once they become established, it seems impossible to do things any other way.

However, perhaps because it was *her nature*, as Quim said, or simply because the desire to test boundaries is all too human, Dolores told lies, little white lies, probably just to prove to herself that she could. And maybe to guard a tiny spec of something vital that has neither shape nor form and which we usually call freedom. They were insignificant transgressions. Smiling coyly when she wanted something. Saying she was going to the hairdresser and then stopping first by a shop or bar, or even a church, which always felt as safe and cosy as a mother's womb. These minor peccadilloes afforded Dolores the thrill of breaking her promise; she had no bad intentions, she was just chasing the ineffable joy of indulging her wishes, even if they were modest.

Sometimes, she came back with a gift for Quim. A cheesecake. A box of white handkerchiefs. A gilt letter opener with a handle in the shape of a rampant lion. A silk scarf, a pack of computer disks, a bottle of bourbon. Quim was suspicious at first, he could see no reason for the gifts, but as they became more frequent, he accepted them gratefully, becoming childishly excited by the sight of the parcels, and he praised her good taste. 'It's all my doing, young lady; if it weren't for me, you'd still choose plaid shirts.' He also got in the habit of buying her small presents when he went out alone. He would return with a bottle of perfume, stockings with intricate jacquard patterns, a box of stationary paper with a trim of purple flowers, cream tarts, marron glacé, a gold chain for Victòria's pendant, which had turned white, a bouquet of flowers, easy-to-remove mascara for those translucent eyelashes that made her eyes look small, a pair of manicure scissors ... Joaquim was unaware that, while his were innocent gifts, hers were the product of the mischievous detours she took in order to contravene the permissions he granted.

One day, however, Dolores went to wait for Ramon to get off work at the factory. She said she was going to collect a jacket from the dry cleaners, but the jacket was already in her car, wrapped in plastic and with the pins still in it. She went to meet Ramon on a whim, just for the pleasure of doing something forbidden. She was only there for a moment, she was *just passing by* ... Ramon suggested they go hunting for wild mushrooms the following Sunday in Montseny, and Dolores replied that the poor mountain chain was spoiled enough as it was, with crowds of people combing the entire countryside in an absurd foraging frenzy. What a shame, Ramon said. Wild mushrooms were so good! He mentioned he'd been given a raise, and he would treat her to the best hot chocolate in the world at a café he knew. The whole thing was so innocent. It was nothing at all.

That Saturday, Ramon came over to the flat for dinner and brought a movie that Dolores was interested in seeing. After dinner, they all sat down to watch it together. Dolores scarcely remembered their brief encounter at the factory, but Ramon, unaware of the mess he was getting her in, mentioned the conversation they had had about going to Montseny. The expression on Quim's face did not change, his eyes remained fixed on the television screen, but out of the corner of his eye he saw Dolores putting a finger to her lips. Ramon went quiet. Even though Joaquim did not react or say anything later, Dolores knew she'd been found out.

From that day on, Joaquim stalked Dolores with such skill, patience, and determination that she never suspected anything. He kept a rented car in the alleyway behind the apartment building, and he followed her whenever she went out. After that, Dolores's little white lies were all tallied up in Joaquim's unerring memory. He kept an accurate record. His mood did not change, but sometimes, after a moment of distraction, she would catch him staring at her with a sour look on his face and a horizontal crease stretching across his forehead.

And every night, for more than half an hour, he watched her sleep. One night Dolores awoke on her own, drowsy enough to not be startled to find Joaquim's hazy silhouette in the dark. She lay perfectly still, her eyes only half open, and she saw his scowling face, the feverish attention, those pain-filled eyes that were like a gash, an open wound. Her whole body was shaking by the time he left her bedroom. She could not fall asleep again. She had a strange presentiment, a dark omen that she struggled to banish from her mind. The foreboding, vague and heavy, was rooted deep within her, and she could not rid herself of it.

23
THE FIFTH STEP (DESCENDING): LEVEL (B)

JON CARNISSER HELD A COOKING PRONG WITH A LAMB CHOP over the lit fireplace. Dolores rubbed some garlic on a piece of toast that was so hot she dropped it. Joaquim opened a bottle of wine using a winged corkscrew. They were celebrating Dolores's nineteenth birthday. Quim had given her a large diamond ring, and every now and then she smiled and held it up as if the precious stone were a magic mirror, and then her face caught the refracted glow of the fire.

'You know, I once had a ring that was very similar to yours,' Quim said. 'The stone wasn't as large, but the diamond was quite pure, and it cost what to me was a fortune, because I was poor as a church mouse.'

'Were you really poor at one time, Quim?'

'Absolutely!'

'Go on,' Jon said, 'tell us what you're dying to say: you're a self-made man, nobody gave you anything. It's hard to believe, but no one is prepared to admit that what they have, whether it be talent or fortune, originated from any source other than themselves. It's called human vanity, which has no beginning and no end. Like time itself.'

'The older you get,' Quim said, 'the more you dish out cheap philosophy. Couldn't you be a little more original and stop parroting such annoying platitudes?'

'Fine. Here's an original question for you. How the hell did you get your hands on this ring that you're describing?'

'I found it,' Quim said.

Jon Carnisser burst out laughing; he placed the cooked lamb chop on a plate and skewered a raw one. Quim blushed a little, just a hint of wine-coloured rosiness that had nothing to do with the warmth of the fire.

'All right, then. I stole it.'

'You? No!' Dolores said, pretending to be scandalized.

'I did a lot of stupid things in my youth, but hear me out. I told myself that I could get at least a hundred dollars for the ring. So I went to one of those jewellers who don't have a storefront but work out of a flat with a sign on the balcony. I wasn't so naive as to believe the jeweller would be honest, but I figured that maybe a hundred dollars … it was worth more than a thousand, so it wasn't too much to expect.'

'How much did he offer you?'

'Nothing! He said it was fake, though I was sure it was valuable, I knew enough about precious stones and had examined it carefully. He called it costume jewellery. I protested, and in a show of feigned generosity the jeweller offered me ten dollars for the setting around the stone, which he said was well crafted and could be reused.'

'So you went to another jeweller,' Jon said.

'I did not. Having laid eyes on such a fine stone, the man wasn't likely to let it slip away. I knew that every jeweller kept a gun under the counter. If I refused to sell the diamond to him, he would use his weapon on me and say I had tried to steal the stone. I put on a face of resigned disappointment, and just as he was reaching for his money box, I grabbed the ring and flew down the stairs.'

'And headed to another jeweller?'

'Damnit, Jon, you are such a bore! There was no way I could take it to another jeweller; they're all in cahoots. As soon as I turned around, he would've phoned a couple of his friends, who would've alerted others in turn. Those are the rules of engagement, and nothing can be done about it. But I needed the money, and above all I wanted to have it my way. I was young and full of bravado.'

Quim glanced discreetly at Dolores, who was salting the cooked lamb chops. When she raised her hand to look at her ring, her skin was splashed with new freckles, small diamond sequins that glowed like sparks from the fire.

'I was so furious,' Quim said. 'I walked around in a stew, wondering how to get back at that scoundrel of a jeweller. Then I had an idea, a very good idea that turned out beautifully. I headed to my local police station.'

'No way!'

'Yes! A gutsy move, and not without risk. It felt good to take a gamble, to dare ... So I got to the precinct and told them that I'd found a ring on the pavement. I asked if they had a lost and found office. Bear in mind that I was young, and forgive me for saying so, but I was quite good-looking and smartly dressed. I had a strong accent, sure, though not as strong an accent as Dolores has; she still can't pronounce her t's in Catalan. But I had good manners. On seeing this honest young foreigner, the officer who assisted me smiled sympathetically and made a little speech about one's civic duty and that kind of thing. Then he started taking down my details. The place was noisy, but it felt as if it was just the two of us there, me and Officer Spencer, sitting at that desk. He gave me a fatherly smile as he wrote down my information. I had a decent job then and a fixed address or I wouldn't have even considered going to the police. He asked me why I hadn't kept the ring. I pretended to be the clueless guy who thinks he's clever. I winked at him and told him that I'd been tempted, finders keepers and so on, and that I had gone to a jeweller and been offered ten dollars for it. Shameful, trying to swindle the poor sod who is only acting in good faith. That's how I ended up bringing it to the police station, I said. I didn't want to deal with jewellers. I told Officer Spencer that I had once worked in a jewellery store, which of course was a lie, but I couldn't let the police know how I had acquired my knowledge. I said the ring was worth more than a thousand dollars. His eyes flashed with excitement; never again have I seen such naked greed on someone's face.'

'Take a look at Dolores,' Jon said. 'If we don't hurry up with dinner, she might start eating her ring!'

'Not sure what good that would do me!' Dolores said. 'We all know where it would end up.'

'Don't be common, Senyoreta! So I pressed my case,' Joquim continued, 'and I planted the idea in the officer's head that a jeweller wouldn't dare to swindle a copper. I made it seem like it was his idea. We could go fifty-fifty.'

'Shameless!' Dolores said.

'What do you think, Jon? Was I the shameless party, or was it the jeweller or the policeman, or maybe all three of us? It worked like a charm. If you had seen the jeweller's face when I showed up with a uniformed officer. Pale as a sheet, he was, babbling away. He swore that his initial appraisal had been an honest mistake; his eyesight wasn't what it once had been. He gave us three hundred dollars for it, a lot of money at the time. Ah! The copper was true to his word: we went fifty-fifty as agreed. He even offered to help me out if any lowlife ever tried to scam me again.'

The following day Dolores went out. She said she needed some trainers so she could play squash with Quim. Tennis was boring. Joaquim trailed her in the rented car. By the time he found a place to park, Dolores was already leaving the store with a shoebox under her arm. But then she didn't go home. Joaquim followed her and double parked on the street; he watched from inside the car, his gaze trained on her as she entered a jewellery store in the centre of town. She was there for some time and re-emerged looking like a well-fed cat that was licking its whiskers. That little swine had just had the ring appraised and seemed really satisfied with the result. He had given her the idea the previous night when he talked about the policeman and the jeweller.

Joaquim was always home before Dolores arrived; whenever he saw her turning the car around and preparing to head back uptown toward the flat, he would speed up and rush ahead. When Dolores got home that afternoon, Joaquim pretended he had been reading. Squash was a tough sport, he told her. Dolores lifted her chin, as she always did when someone challenged her, and said that she would beat him;

he might be stronger, but she was more agile. He would see. She showed him her new trainers.

'You were gone a long time,' Quim said.

'Ugh, the shops are so busy on Saturday!'

It was still early for dinner, so Joaquim suggested they read for a while. Dolores picked up the first book she came across and sat down with a sigh. Joaquim was watching her and noticed that she wasn't turning the pages but was smiling to herself with thinly veiled rapacity. He wanted to slap her. The little traitor. The bloody liar. All at once, Dolores stared at the page in front of her and gasped. She sat up and exclaimed: 'Look what it says here, Quim! How beautiful, how well expressed!' She showed him the book. The silly girl had picked up Seneca's *Letters from a Stoic* to pretend she was reading. She was all deception and lies, it was all play-acting with her. *Mistrust justifies betrayal.* That was the line in the book that she pointed out to him. The words pummelled Joaquim and reverberated in his mind. He read them three times, then gazed at Dolores. They exchanged a dark look. Her eyes said: See? The more you insist on watching me, the more I must deceive you. And his: Why do you hurt me, when I am so good to you?

The next day, Joaquim played a terrible game of squash, and Dolores bragged about beating him. In the shower, Joaquim ran his hands over his saggy skin, the white hairs on his body, his flabby belly and lax muscles, and he felt the bitter sting of time. If only he were Faust. Oh, if he were Faust!

Loneliness was once good company. I enjoyed being the ruler, the master and lord of my kingdom. I took pleasure in cynicism and amused myself by mocking the gullible. And I flaunted the melancholy knowledge of the wise, of those who understand that we exist, at most, in a vegetative state. You weren't even pretty. You didn't inspire lavish wet dreams or fantasies of joyful orgies. I made you. And I cannot bear this much longer. Hatred. Contemptuous idleness. Even betrayal. These I can endure. But this impotent rage gnaws at me, and I writhe in pain, my disembowelled pride like the entrails of a dead man, the taste in my mouth bitter, my eyes on fire ... I burn. I burn!

It was you who created me, and then you tossed me into the fire and scattered the ashes!

24
THE FOURTH STEP (DESCENDING): QUADRANT (A)

A CURIOUS THING HAPPENED. ONE SATURDAY AFTERNOON Ramon showed up at the flat and asked to speak to Joaquim alone, just the two of them. They went into Quim's study. Dolores stared at the closing door feeling disoriented. What could her friend possibly want? And why couldn't she listen as well?

She got on her computer and started playing a boring game that Ramon loved. She nibbled on the multicoloured candy she kept in a large bowl, the aniseed-flavoured sweets crunching in her mouth. That first taste was the best, afterwards the candy paste became goopy. She gobbled them by the handful to spite Joaquim because he had told her that she liked sweets too much and she should be careful and look after her teeth. An hour later, Dolores's curiosity was stronger than her patience and she came out of her room to see what the story was with Ramon.

Joaquim was in the living room reading the newspaper.

'And Ramon?' she said.

'Ramon? He left some time ago.'

'He didn't tell me. What did he want?'

'Nothing, just to have a chat.'

Dolores picked up the cushion she had been working on earlier, sat down next to Joaquim, and started embroidering. Joaquim's face gave nothing away. He seemed neither happy nor displeased. She, on the other hand, was filled with a distinct feeling of sadness. Ramon had forgotten about her, and he was supposedly her friend, not Joaquim's.

'You know what, Quim?'

'Hmm.'

'I have no roots.'

'Neither do I.'

'I can't really say that I'm from Colorado Moon any more, and I'm not from here either. I don't belong anywhere.'

Quim put down the newspaper and looked at Dolores.

'So what if you don't belong anywhere?' he said. 'I don't either.'

'That's not true. You're from here. Otherwise, why would you come back?'

'Some people leave just for the pleasure of being able to return. Don't you know that?'

'I remember less and less about Colorado Moon. I hardly think about it any more.'

'Better that way,' Quim said. 'It means you've found your place here. Some people never adapt, though I've never understood why.'

'But everyone needs roots,' Dolores said. 'Not having roots is like saying, oh, I don't know ... it's like saying you don't know who you are.'

I have no roots. No roots, no trunk, no branches, no

leaves. I have nothing.

'Enough of this nonsense,' Joaquim said. 'Now let me read in peace.'

Dolores got up and went to her room; she sat down in front of the mirror, put her elbows on the dressing table, and rested her chin on her hands. She was quite pretty. She liked her looks. But Serafí had never contacted her again. Wasn't she attractive enough? Was she that bad in bed? Hadn't he enjoyed himself? And Joaquim was still watching her at night ... but why? It was so creepy. And now Ramon, her one friend, the only friend she had, was asking to talk to Joaquim alone.

She was at her lowest point, feeling utterly dejected, when through her mind flashed a thought as scintillating as the tail of a comet. It was like a mental thunderbolt. Dolores smiled. Could it be that Ramon fancied her? Maybe he knew that everything had to go through Joaquim and had wanted to talk to him first. She blushed. Dimples formed on her cheeks. She stamped her feet, she raised her arms over her head and fluffed her hair.

It was true that Ramon was a little younger than she was, but he certainly didn't act younger. And he had a job, although Joaquim didn't care very much about that. She knew he liked Ramon; they wouldn't even be friends if Quim didn't approve. But shouldn't Ramon have spoken to her first? And Joaquim, what had he said to Ramon? He didn't look sullen, nor did he seem happy. But there was nothing else it could be, it had to be what she thought it was. How did she feel about it? Ah, Ramon was the best! She felt comfortable around him. His skin was probably warm, his hands strong, his lips soft as flour, his kiss passionate. Dolores lay on the bed with her hands behind her head and fantasised about Ramon, gradually becoming aware of just how much she yearned to feel his caress.

She came out of her room and asked Joaquim if they should start thinking about dinner. She walked up behind him and tickled him until he laughed. Over supper, she studied him and tested the waters, posing indirect questions about Ramon. But Joaquim wouldn't say a word.

A week passed, a whole week that seemed to have a thousand days and countless hours. And still more days went by with Dolores feeling anxious and Joaquim being affable, and Ramon entirely missing in action. And then Ramon phoned and suggested they meet up the following Sunday, maybe they could go to the café he'd mentioned one day.

It's happening. It's happening. It's happening.

The café was too crowded to get in, as were all the bars they tried. Dolores was wearing a new dress. Ramon had on a tie and didn't look like himself. They finally found a rather sleazy bar where people gave them nasty looks. There were red lamps at each table, and the dim lighting created an intimate atmosphere.

It's happening, it's happening now.

Ramon didn't say anything. He poked the crushed ice in his glass with a straw, like a woodpecker tapping the bark of a tree, his head down, his attention drifting. Dolores realized she had never been able to confide in anyone; she got a lump in her throat whenever she tried to describe Joaquim's weirdness or the thick web of fear and mistrust that stood between them. Or bound them together. But she really wanted to be open with Ramon. She began slowly.

'Quim is a strange man, isn't he?'

'That he is. He knows so much about life.'

'Victòria used to say that he's a bit mental.'

'Maybe that's true. But he's honourable.'

'He controls everything I do.'

'I'd sure like it if someone watched over me like that.'

'If you knew what he ... '

'All I know for sure is what I can see with my own eyes.'

'Remember Vulgar? Well, he didn't run away. He ... '

The words died in her throat; she didn't know how to articulate her thoughts. She realised that what she had to say would sound absurd. There was a long pause. Ramon stopped pecking at the ice and downed the entire drink in one gulp.

'I wanted to talk to you, Dolores.'

It's happening. It's happening!

'I'm listening, more than you are to me.'

'You think I don't listen to you?'

'You don't. I'm trying to talk to you and tell you things and you aren't really paying attention.'

'What you are trying to do is criticize Quim; he must've told you off or something, and I won't have you speaking badly about him.'

'Wow. I didn't realize the two of you were such good friends.'

'Listen, Dolores, your father is a good man. And I am deeply indebted to him.'

'You?'

'Yes, me. You know the factory? Well, I was in a tough spot. They were laying people off right and left and basing their decision solely on seniority. I was in a real bind. I was practically out on the street. And here I had just been given a raise! It was my mother's idea. She said to me, why don't you tell Senyor Simon? He has a lot of connections. She might not seem so bright, my mother, but she was right on the money. I explained the situation to Quim, and the next day, the very next day, I got a call from the personnel department, and they told me not to worry. I was staying. When I talked to Joaquim, he mentioned that he knew the owner of the company quite well. But why should he do me a favour? Why? Because he's a decent, upstanding man, a genuinely good person. That's why. So, I won't have you criticizing him, especially over something trivial. If you only knew how lucky you are!'

That dimly lit bar was no place for shared confidences, but a sinister venue where dirt accumulated in dark corners. Dolores felt helpless and lowered her head.

'What did you want to tell me?' she said in a faint voice.

'Oh, right. The thing is ... we're good friends, you and me, and I think you should know that I have a girlfriend now, and I'm very... well, I'm very taken with her. She's ... she's wonderful!'

Her name was Virgínia, and she was studying to be a teacher. She was crazy about children; she had brown hair and was good at drawing. She dressed simply, but everything looked good on her because she had natural grace. Ramon had met her through his Uncle Martí, who was a builder and earned a pile of money; she had been babysitting their four-year-old boy. Ramon said he was happy, so very happy.

Dolores wanted to be a good friend, so she just squeezed his hand.

That night when she turned in, she locked her bedroom door from the inside. She did not go to sleep. She had sneaked in a bottle of gin that was practically full and got drunk by herself. She was resolute about it, as if fulfilling an obligation. She didn't shed a tear.

It took her three days to get over the headache and to realise that Joaquim was eyeing her with concern.

CHAPTER IX – OCCULTUM

25
THE FOURTH STEP (DESCENDING): QUADRANT(B)

JACINT ESCRIVÀ WAS OFTEN AT THE FLAT. IT WAS PLAIN THAT he was courting Dolores, and she accepted it half-heartedly, with an apathy that spilled into her daily life and her thoughts. She tried to hold on to her memories of Colorado Moon, but she felt them slipping away, as if they belonged to another person, someone whose life had begun the day she knocked on Joaquim Simon's door.

Joaquim was no longer trying to put off the young doctor, but courteously accepting his visits with broad, friendly smiles. He even seemed to be encouraging him, nudging him towards Dolores. Maybe Joaquim's nightly visits to her bedside—how many had there been?—did not mean all that much. It's not that he wanted her for himself. Maybe all he really wanted was to control her every move, possibly even her thoughts. He needed to be fully in charge.

Jacint was a quiet, pensive fellow who told bad jokes at the wrong moment to mask his diffidence. But Dolores sensed an inner strength in him, a sturdiness as solid as the trunk of a tree. She so wanted to be able to speak and be heard;

her need to tell someone about the state of bewilderment she was in ran as deep as the sea. She realised that she was losing hold of her past and slowly settling into a life of captivity where she belonged to another person. The terror this evoked in her was all-consuming, hard and viscous like a beetle; it left her wide-eyed and gasping for air. She tried to be rational about it. She compiled a list of the advantages of submitting to her father's will, fully recognizing that being controlled by someone else made some things easier. Her nascent friendship with Jacint brought forth this inner turmoil, all the mixed-up emotions and overworked thoughts that were like a thick foul jelly, yet at the same time it spurred new hope in her, like a door left ajar at the end of a corridor, allowing a sliver of sunlight through the crack.

Jacint seemed to prefer spending his afternoons at the flat to being out on the town. Dancing and loud noises were not for him. He loved the medical profession and expounded on it at length; he told them all about his projects. But if he ever glanced at Dolores his words died in his throat, and when their eyes met an electric field seemed to absorb his thoughts. Joaquim was amused by this, even invigorated.

If the young ones decided to go out, Joaquim conversed with Jacint while Dolores changed clothes.

'So, are you planning on starting your own practice?' Quim said.

'My father's practice is doing quite well, and I'd like to benefit from that. Starting from scratch is ... ' Jacint clicked his tongue and shook his head.

Life's inescapable challenges.

'What about Dolores ... you like her, don't you?'

Joaquim tried to be friendly, he tried to use guy talk to draw Jacint out and establish a good rapport.

'She's not like any other girl I know. She's ... special,' Jacint said. 'It's as if she can see through walls and objects, and even peer into your brain. She sees right through people. She's a good person, clever and sweet without being silly or stuck-up or weak. She's strong on the outside and gentle on the inside.'

'Just like a liqueur-filled bonbon. Delicious! Bite into the dark, bitter chocolate shell and you taste the sweetness of its molten inner secrets.'

'I wouldn't want you to think ... I don't really see her like that, as an object of desire.'

'You're not attracted to her?'

'Oh, yes, of course I am! But that's not all, there's so much more. What I mean is—'

Tongue-tied and mortified, the young man fled with Dolores as soon as she finished getting dressed. This was a recurring thing. He didn't share his feelings with Dolores. She, on the other hand, was eager to tell Jacint everything, as if he were her personal physician.

Later, Joaquim would use a similar friendly approach with Dolores.

Was it fun?

Did you go to the concert?

Good, good.

So, tell me, do you like Jacint?

'I like him fine,' Dolores said. 'He's nice. A good person.'

'But do you see him as a friend or something more?'

'I'm not sure. I think he's serious about me though.'

'And how do you feel about that?'

'I don't feel anything. I never do. I try to live my life and take advantage of the good things, and I rid myself of the rest.'

'Do you like Jacint or not?'

'I don't like anything in general. I don't dislike anything either. But I'm comfortable around Jacint; he's good company and he listens to me.'

There's nothing to listen to because I have nothing to say, or too much to say, because I'm ashamed to admit that I do not know who I am, and because talking about Quim is always inappropriate. Everything intimidates me.

'He is very self-assured,' Dolores said.

Joaquim had to go out of town. He was considering becoming a partner in an upscale hotel that was being built on the coast. The project needed capital, and he was asked to invest, but he wanted to see it for himself before making a decision. It wasn't exactly a leisure trip, so it didn't make sense to take Dolores with him. He would be gone for three or four days, and she would be on her own. She could do whatever she liked while he was away, with one caveat. Joaquim raised his finger and told Dolores that she was not to go out with Jacint or have him over to the house.

'That's all I'm asking,' he said. 'It's not much. I do like the boy. I think he can be good for you, Dolores, but I don't want the two of you playing like mice while the cat is away. I'll only be gone three or four days. You can manage. I would be terribly upset to find out that you had met up with him without my knowing the how, the when, and the where. Give him whatever excuse you like or tell him the truth. I don't care.'

Dolores paced the flat and traipsed across Barcelona alone. She didn't feel like cheating, so she didn't see Jacint; she honoured Joaquim's request. She trudged on, allowing the air to hold her, and her feet took her from the seaport to Gràcia, from Horta to Plaça d'Espanya. She ended up exhausted but calm.

She wandered about the flat in a state of apathy and entered Quim's study. She poked her nose in his papers, opened drawers and read things she didn't understand and others she did understand but which held no interest for her. And then she found the letter under a black leather folder. Jack Thurber's letter, still in its envelope. Joaquim had mentioned this letter, but she'd never seen it.

Dear Quim,

I'm getting old and I often get things mixed up. I thought I had a good nose, but it turns out I'm no good. I'm all washed up. Michael Gardner was one of us, and for him to be killed like that ... but I had it all wrong. Apparently, he had a debt with the mob and tried to get out of paying it, so they bumped him off. I sent you Gardner's daughter thinking she was a dead woman walking. That man had done such stupid things, and he always ran his mouth. I was sure it was a death sentence for her ... can't do much about it now! No one is after the girl, there's no plot against her, nothing sinister at all. Forgive me for tasking you with such a pointless assignment. She's free to use her own name and come home, though she won't find much of one any more, not since Gardner was killed and she ran off. There is no need for her to keep hiding or pretend she's Hispanic. Write to me, won't you, and tell me what you've done with her.

And forgive this old fool for muddling things up, but don't waste your time seeking compensation. I'm flat broke.

Remember the old days? We were something, you and I ...
Warmly,
Jack Thurber

Dolores stared at the letter as if it had nothing to do with her. She tried to process what it meant. Michael Gardner was her father. No one was looking for her. And it made no sense for her to continue to use the name Dolores Simon. Nothing bound her to Joaquim; he had deceived her in order to hold on to her. Dominate her. Or maybe even because he loved her.

Dolores decided to leave. She burst into her room to pack a suitcase. She wouldn't even leave a note. But when she opened her closet and saw all her clothes neatly lined up, her stomach dropped. Where would she go? She didn't know how to stop being Dolores. Or who Dorothy was, the girl she had been. She didn't know how to live her life without Quim telling her what to do. Her hands clutched the open doors of her closet. She dropped her head and sobbed.

When she managed to calm down, she went to the telephone. She had told Jacint that she was going out of town with Quim for a few days, but she needed to unburden herself. Jacint was a good listener, and even if he struggled to believe her story, he would still listen. She dialled the number.

The trilling sound—bringg bringg bringg—was that of a phone ringing in an empty flat.

Jacint was not home.

26
THE THIRD STEP (DESCENDING): CHISEL (A)

DOLORES WAS FURIOUS AT JOAQUIM.

I am a human being. I am a person, a person. No one can own another human being. I'm a human being. I—

She had intended to brandish Jack Thurber's letter at Joaquim, but he was so cheerful when he got back. If she told him about it, he would likely adopt his usual cavalier attitude and say, Well, what did you expect? That the whole world was after you and there was no hiding place but right here under my roof? Just accept it, Dolores. Accept the fact that you like being with me. And that you are mine, all mine.

She went out with Ramon and his girlfriend. Virginia rested her head on Ramon's shoulder and closed her eyes as if demented, while Ramon just sat there secreting tenderness at the trustful abandon of this girl who wanted to be a teacher and could not even take control of her own person.

Dolores couldn't tell Ramon was happening with Joaquim, just as she hadn't dared to let Jacint know. But that afternoon, while she was out with Ramon and Virginia, she ran into

Serafí. He was with a group of friends who were being loud and boisterous. He immediately took notice of Dolores and kept shooting her knowing glances. No doubt emboldened by her alcohol intake, she flung herself at him. She emulated Virginia and rested her ginger head on his weak shoulders, smelled his aftershave and felt the casual caress of his fingers. They should meet up again, she told him. Just the two of them. Alone. 'I miss you, you know?' she said in a seductive voice.

Serafí suggested a specific date. A friend of his had a flat he could lend him, but it had to be on a Thursday. 'Believe it or not he's got a wait list,' Serafí said. 'Ever since AIDS came on the scene, parents, that strange species called *parents*, keepers of all human offspring, have turned into the secret police. Parents are always afraid, that seems to be the definition of parenthood. Their species is just *so* conservative.' Five o'clock at this address. 'I'll bring drinks,' he said, 'and you bring ... no, don't bring anything, just yourself; that's all I need.' He told her that he remembered her scent, and the silky smoothness of her skin.

Ramon and Virgínia didn't notice any of this, lost as they were in each other's gaze, swimming there, drinking it in like melted ice cream sucked through a straw.

Dolores savoured her revenge even as she made her plans. This was not something fortuitous that suddenly happened, it was thought out well in advance to punish Joaquim. *Fuck the old fucker. Fuck the bastard who deceived me and now holds me down against my will.*

She told Joaquim that she was going out again with Ramon and his girlfriend. Virginia wanted to go to the flea market in Plaça de les Glòries to pick out some furniture; she couldn't stand Ramon's mother, so she and Ramon were moving in together. Dolores didn't realize that Joaquim followed her when she went out, but had she known this, it would have only increased her determination. Her aim was to ridicule and humiliate him. To trample on him. The old bastard.

Joaquim had no idea what Dolores might be doing in that apartment building on Carrer Aribau, so he speculated, weighing all the possibilities that his imagination could conjure. He had asked so little of her, only that she obey him. He parked the car on the pavement outside the building. He could afford to get a fine, but he couldn't afford to lose track of her, that would be a more serious matter. He studied the mailboxes but didn't recognize any of the names. He went home bewildered and sulked for a long time.

Dolores was gone for more than three hours. She seemed different when she came back. Her eyes shone like green embers, her cheeks were flushed, her lips dry. This time there was no telling scent on her, and Joaquim wasn't sure what had happened. Or with whom. Ramon? No. Ramon was honourable, solid, and he owed him a huge favour. Jacint? No, no. Jacint was a gentleman, and serious about Dolores, he wasn't just stringing her along.

Joaquim phoned a friend, who phoned a friend. He was finally given the name of a skilled, overpriced but discreet private investigator, and because Joaquim was a powerful man the detective immediately made time for him. He was a stocky guy with puffy cheeks, a moustache, and a receding hairline, and he wore a signet ring on his middle finger. He scribbled in an ash-coloured notebook, then gave Joaquim an amused nod. This was not a hard one to figure out. Everyone wanted the same. Control. Over a woman, over money, friends, family, business affairs. Control meant power.

A week later, Joaquim had the name of the person renting the flat and of the friend who was allowed to use it, as well as the dates and times when this man and Dolores had met there. The fact that it was again Serafí was an added affront. There was a name for this, recidivism, an aggravating factor in criminal law. And the boy was a fool, a complete moron. She could have done so much better!

He stopped the car outside the door and crouched down to keep Dolores from seeing him when she arrived. Today's excuse for going out was so weak it wasn't even close to being credible. She was no idiot. Either the little bitch was brazenly defying him, or she had lost her mind. Joaquim waited. For hours. Serafí finally showed up and entered the building. Then Dolores appeared and rushed up the stairs. The detective had placed a small hidden camera in the small bedroom of that nondescript flat. Joaquim held the remote control in his hands, he wanted to be the one to obtain irrefutable proof. The camera was pointed toward the bed. Joaquim pressed the on button and gritted his teeth. Then he went home. It would be better to just die, melt away, simply let life escape his body. How he burned with the shame of being alive.

The following day he received a manila envelope with his name on it and nothing else, no return address. A large envelope containing a videotape. He locked himself in his study and, videotape in hand, he froze as painful questions clicked through his mind. He was entitled to this; he had the right. So why did he feel so vicious, so mean? He eyed the envelope as if he was standing at the gates of hell.

The grainy footage started in mid-action: Dolores was naked and rolling around in bed. Big fat tears welled up in Joaquim's eyes, refusing to fall. He pressed rewind and watched the video again. He was nauseous, he kept having to pause the tape. He felt as if he'd been lashed across the face. And debased for his actions, for spying. He'd fallen so low, snooping like that! But how would he put out the fire that consumed him day and night?

Fifteen days later, he had three video recordings. He watched them at night and wept. What a fool he was! Keeping up the façade of a normal home life left him exhausted, spent like an empty bottle of cognac that still holds a strong scent but no spirit.

Look at me, exposed, embittered, old. Look at me now and laugh. I have never practiced destruction. I have not dealt in the mistrust caused by betrayal nor in the greed that feeds disquiet. I am no agitator. I am not wicked. But you are wild water slipping through my fingers. Look at me: a beggar, my hand extended, palm open, stunned to find that it is empty. Mock me, for I am the very image of the fool. Look at me and roar. I am an old man. I am laughable.

At night, he no longer crept into her bedroom to watch her sleep. He played the videotapes over and over, wallowing in his misery, half mad.

Dolores sensed that something was off but was not afraid. Her gaze was hard. She was fed up with Serafí and his idiotic self, and now even her own pleasure struck her as superfluous and routine. It held no interest for her, but she kept going back for more. Fuck you, fuck you, fuck you, she repeated to herself on her way there. She didn't know that Joaquim was watching her, but knowing that what she was doing would hurt him was empowering, and *that* gave her pleasure. He couldn't do anything to her, nothing at all. He couldn't touch her. Again and again, she crawled into that lion's den, though the place itself was immaterial, as inconsequential as Serafí and no doubt his friend as well.

One Saturday evening, Dolores tried to share a funny anecdote with Joaquim, but he dismissed her quite rudely. She gave him an angry stare. She fixed him with that gaze that Jacint said could see through walls and peer into people's brains.

'You whore,' Joaquim said.

Dolores went to her room and returned with a sheet of paper. She had been holding a piece of paper the day she first rang his doorbell, a dirty, frightened little gypsy girl that he took in like a stray cat, one, as it turned out, that liked to use its claws. This, too, was a letter, and it was also from Thurber. Dolores tossed it into Joaquim's lap and stood in front of him, her hands on her hips, a look of contempt on her face. She was filled with hatred. She looked beautiful.

Joaquim recognized the letter as soon as he unfolded the paper. The little thief had ransacked his study. He could have killed her. She stood there silently, hands on her hips, eyes gleaming. He shrank back into his chair, as if recoiling from a scorpion's poisonous stinger. He really wanted to kill her. 'You little whore, you filthy beast,' he muttered, and she heard him. 'I'm leaving, Joaquim,' she told him. Her tone was determined and held no fear.

A rush of panic took over his whole being. He no longer wanted to kill her. He wanted to hold onto her. At any cost.

27
THE THIRD STEP (DESCENDING): CHISEL (B)

JOAQUIM WATCHED DOLORES PACK HER SUITCASE. THE FACT that she was clearly furious gave him hope; a cool-headed, well-thought-out decision was practically set in stone. But a tantrum was like all things in life. Fleeting.

He was smarter than she was. He could change her mind.

'Would you kindly tell me why you are leaving, Dolores?'

She didn't answer, but she blinked as she was leaning over her suitcase, a sign, perhaps, that she was having second thoughts.

'Maybe you should take a piece of paper and write down your reasons for leaving,' Joaquim said. 'You could do it right now. List your grievances. It's a really good exercise; it can keep us from getting carried away by our emotions. Won't you give it a try?'

'I know why I'm leaving!' Dolores said. 'I made the decision days ago when I found the letter. There's no doubt in my mind. All those sermons, all that advice. And all along it was you who was deceiving me!'

'Looking for these?' Joaquim handed Dolores some jumpers that were piled on her desk. 'If that is the case, why not take things one step at a time. Give me your list of reasons. Go on.'

'First of all, you lied.'

'Nonsense! How does that little lie warrant you leaving and giving up such a pleasant and cushy life? Talk about overreacting, Dolores!'

'It's not just any lie, what you did was despicable, disgusting, it was—'

'All right, let's talk about it then. Why do you suppose I deceived you? What reasons do you think I had?'

'It's as clear as day! You wanted to keep me here.'

'And why would I want you to stay?'

'I don't know. I don't know!'

'Does that mean I hate you?' Joaquim said. 'Does it mean I don't care about you? Why would one person want to hold on to someone else?'

'Fine. You love me so much and want to be near me,' Dolores said. 'But to use such lies to accomplish your goals, you, a man who fancies himself above reproach, always preaching about loyalty, about being truthful and forthright. I could spit on you right now!'

'You already have, in a way. You went with Serafí to get back at me. If it didn't hurt so much (*Oh, the pain*) I would say we're even now. The difference being that I acted out of affection, and you out of hatred.'

'Who says I've been with Serafí? Besides, you have no right to interfere. I can do whatever I want with whomever I want.'

'Are you denying you had sex with Serafí?'

'Yes.'

Joaquim grabbed Dolores by the wrist and dragged her to his study. He inserted a videotape in the player and shoved Dolores into a chair. A few minutes later Dolores was covering her face in shame and refused to watch any more. Joaquim paused the video and lifted her chin.

'Why do you lie?' he said. 'Why do you insist on lying to me?'

'You spied on me, you spied on me! You're mad! A sick man!'

'Listen, Dolores, listen to me carefully. I took you in when you were a feral creature. I wanted to make you into, oh, I don't know, I wanted to turn you into a masterpiece! You have the makings of one, and I knew how to go about it. And look at you now: no one from your old life would recognize you, and it's only been a few short years. I've taken care of you. If I've made mistakes or allowed myself to get carried away, I apologize. I'm sorry. I ask you to forgive me. But I did it for you, Dolores. What would I get out of it? Can't you see? Transforming a person requires discipline, it takes effort. At the end of the day, I never denied you anything. Did I?'

'How dare you! You killed Vulgar. You locked me up with his dead body and you left. I'm not saying you didn't do anything for me, but you've also been cruel and unfair.'

'I knew it. I knew this would happen. I swear to God that I never meant to kill him, Dolores. I only wanted to inflict a superficial wound. Please believe me, Dolores. I wanted to drive some sense into you, to make you reconsider your actions. I wanted to awaken the tenderness you felt for the poor dog, and maybe then, through him—'

'You swear to God? You don't believe in anything!'

'I believe in God.'

'No father watches over his child the way you do, controlling her, punishing her the way you punish me.'

'No father loves as I do.'

Dolores bowed her head in defeat. She felt like giving up and resigning herself to her circumstances. A little dot of white light bounced around inside her brain. Joaquim's silhouette seemed to glow in the dark.

'Do you love me, Quim?' she muttered without looking up.

Joaquim flew into a rage.

'Just go!' he yelled. 'Go if you want to but leave me be! I don't want anything from you!'

He stormed out of the study and slammed the door. Dolores sat down, confused. Maybe he was crazy and cruel. But he loved her. What agony, what joy, to be the object of such feverish devotion!

She did what he asked. She took time to reflect. Assess matters. Analyse her reasons. She felt anguished, and so utterly subjugated. Joaquim didn't allow her any breathing room, and yet she was also happy with him. Dolores went back and forth from one extreme to the other, considering everything from all possible angles. She felt like a rat trapped in a maze, going round in circles and unable to find her way out.

Dolores looked around the flat and assumed that Joaquim was in his bedroom. She put her eye to the keyhole. He was sitting up in bed with his head on his knees. He was the image of defeat. A pang of compassion gnawed at her. She headed to the kitchen and set about preparing a delicious dinner. Salmon mousse and roasted lamb chops. A Côte-Rôtie that she chose especially. She laid the table with the linen tablecloth and the good china. Why do we have such need to redeem ourselves?

At the end of the day, she had nowhere else to go.

She was smarter than he was. She could change his mind.

She knocked on his bedroom door. 'Dinner's on the table,' she said in a neutral tone.

Joaquim stood at the door to the dining room; he scrutinized the table and then Dolores's face, smiling with his eyes. Then he gave a slow nod and sat down.

They had finished the first course when Dolores broke the silence.

'I want you to know that I don't care about Serafí.'

'You only wanted to punish me.'

'I wanted to hurt you, and I still do.'

'So why does it bother you that I made those tapes? The idea was for me to suffer, no?'

'It made me happy to think I was fooling you, disobeying you. I didn't know you were spying on me.'

'Evidently, you are as twisted as I am.'

'I am your creation, right?'

'I'm beginning to have my doubts. More and more. And I do have some good qualities as well, you know?'

'So do I.'

The pall of silence that followed was punctuated by the sound of clinking cutlery and lasted until dessert.

'Quim, I'm suffocating.'

'But just think—'

'Let me finish. If instead of imposing, ordering, punishing, you simply asked—'

'This kind of thinking is a trap, Dolores. It's a fallacy! We all see ourselves as basically good, but evil lurks in every human being.'

'I'm not sure about that. But I think that if you had said to me, Look Dolores, all that about your father is in the past now, you are not in danger, but I'd really like you to stay. Oh, Quim! Can't you see? I like it here with you. I have no reason to leave!'

'Sooner or later, a Serafí type will come along and start blathering on about your rights, your options. Everyone, absolutely everyone talks about rights, but only rarely about responsibilities.'

'But why this desire to control me?'

Joaquim didn't immediately respond, and when he finally did, Dolores could scarcely remember what her question had been. He spoke slowly, almost in a whisper.

'I don't think there's any other way to love.'

That night, Joaquim slipped into Dolores's bedroom to watch her sleep. But her eyes were wide open. The two of them looked at each other for a long time without saying anything, and then they both smiled. When she fell asleep, he gently ran his fingers across the bottom of the bedspread. Then he tiptoed away as silently as if he were made of air.

CHAPTER X – LAPIDEM

28
THE SECOND STEP (DESCENDING): GAVEL (A)

A FEELING OF MALAISE CREPT INTO THAT UPTOWN FLAT IN Barcelona. The air seemed foul, the walls mouldy, and its occupants' words were lifeless, their unseeing eyes shot daggers. This time the weariness did not subside. It was too late.

They were two silent creatures, spying on each other, distrustful, yet needing one another, like microbes that cannot subsist without harming their host. Any tenderness between them had vanished, that delicate fabric had frayed beyond repair, and they had become locked in a battle whose sole satisfaction, as in all battles, lay in being able to claim victory. Such is the boundless stupidity of humankind.

It required willpower to see them through their days, for in their brittle stoicism they had abdicated their true strength. Victòria's larger-than-life presence had been an open window onto the world, and this was shut when she had been felled. Ramon no longer came to the apartment; he had the full and busy life of someone who has climbed a mountain and now stands surveying the landscape below, taking it all in, claiming it for himself. Only the years—sometimes not even the years—would eventually turn this view from the summit into an unattainable dream.

Jon Carnisser continued to visit, but he was ailing, despondent and melancholy. Cancer was eating away at him, and he was not ready to die; no one is, not even an insect without a sense of self. He was afraid of finding himself locked in a prison of pain. He said he could face his demise, but in reality, he could not, and when the sting of physical suffering reminded him of the fleeting hour, he recoiled in terror.

Jacint also stopped by from time to time, and then Dolores and Joaquim would put on a show of being good hosts, but a mantle of frost enveloped their words and their gaze. On that particular stage, in that corner of the great theatre, the actors read through their script but offered a weak performance.

Dolores never went out any more. She had abandoned her needlepoint project and no longer read. She had no interest in cooking or even in eating; she lost weight and had dark circles under her blue eyes. Hands folded, she sat staring into midair, plunged into a well of nothingness, a blank page, an empty mind. It's not easy to sit still without thinking about anything. That kind of void is only reserved for the dead.

Such were the circumstances when one afternoon, one very noisy afternoon, with whistles and sirens sounding in the street, perhaps from an accident—but what did Dolores care about that?—the face of her friend Thomas from Colorado Moon came to her, clear and precise. Pulling on the thread of memory, she tried to retrieve Dorothy's old life. The life of the girl she had been. Thomas would be quite different now. Maybe he didn't even live in Colorado Moon any more. Maybe he wouldn't remember her. She felt a ferocious need to get in touch with him and try to build a bridge, even if a shabby one, to a time that was quickly slipping away from her.

She took a piece of paper and wrote a letter to her friend, so distant and tenuous in her mind. She asked about the old gang, about her father's house, about Emmy—was she still a maid in the Big House? That's what they called the only house left from the town's heyday as a copper mining centre. Emmy was forty years old when Dorothy ran away. She lived in the Big House, which belonged to a couple whose children had long since moved out. The Grellets? Or maybe the Grellers? Dolores wasn't sure. They couldn't afford to keep Emmy on, but she chose to stay. The house was falling apart, the woodwork was rotting away and in urgent need of repair. But Emmy, in her white apron and lace mobcap, conferred a touch of distinction on the old couple, who were poor but well shod and well dressed, always in their tattered fur-trimmed coats that were brown with age. It was thinking about Thomas that had reminded Dolores of Emmy. That huge house could hold a lot of people. If she were to return ... if she went back to Colorado Moon and found someone living in her father's old house, maybe she could ask Emmy if, in exchange for helping out ... only until she could find something, of course ... the time it would take for her to get back on her feet ... Dolores was surprised by her own thoughts, they seemed to come from far away or deep within, as if the mind she did her best to control and restrain had nevertheless been working behind the scenes to offer up plans about which she had been kept in the dark. She finished the letter and wrote the address, strangely proud to still remember it. She licked the envelope and stamps and told herself that she would post it at once, lest Quim find it and confiscate it. This is what things had come to. This is how low she had allowed herself to fall.

Unfortunately, the phone rang. Unfortunately, the delivery man from the grocer's was laid up in bed with an illness and their order would not be dispatched that day. Unfortunately, Dolores decided to pop down to collect the shopping herself and she didn't think to take the letter and post it on her way.

Unfortunately, the door to Dolores's room was left open and Joaquim looked in and spotted the letter. The dishwasher had just stopped, and he used the steam coming from it to open the envelope. He read the letter, sealed the envelope again, and left it where he had found it. He sat down in the rocking chair that faced the entrance. Simmering with rage, his fingers interlaced, he stared at the door.

Dolores came home panting, carrying a heavy shopping load.

'So, you want this Emmy to let you stay with her,' Joaquim told her. 'You've decided to run away.'

Dolores denied this, and she wasn't exactly lying, for she hadn't fully realised that her decision had been made.

'And you're thinking that one of your lovers, this Thomas, will join you there.'

Again, she denied it.

'Rip up the letter. Now.'

Dolores didn't take the grocery bags into the kitchen; they were left in the entrance hall looking incongruous and out of place. She headed to her room and reappeared with the letter, which she held up and tore asunder without taking her eyes off Joaquim's darkened gaze. The pieces sailed through the air and floated down like snowflakes on the gleaming tile floor.

'I can always write another one,' she said in a neutral tone, her arms resting at her side, her head held high.

Joaquim gave a contemptuous laugh. He stood up from the rocking chair and went about locking all the doors. Then he collected the keys and slipped them into his pocket. They stood facing each other in a standoff, and at that precise moment Dolores became fully conscious of her decision to leave. The realization came quietly, no excitement, no hysterics. There was no turning back.

Joaquim must have sensed this.

'I know what I must do,' he said. 'You leave me no other option, Dolores.'

He dragged her to her bedroom and pushed her down on the bed. Then he left. Dolores didn't move. She didn't care what he did to her. Sooner or later, one way or another, she would be free. Poor Quim, there was nothing he could do about it.

Fuck him.

Joaquim came back into the room holding a syringe. Terrified, Dolores tried to flee, but he grabbed her. 'If you're not still,' he said, 'this will hurt, but it won't harm you; you'll just feel a little groggy.' The shot was like a long stab in the arm. Seconds later, everything wobbled, the walls crumbled. She was only dimly aware of being tied up with a rope, of Joaquim leaving and furiously slamming the front door.

Everything was dark when Dolores woke up. Her wrists were chafed from the rope. She was woozy, as if she were drunk, and her dry mouth burned like it was full of desert sand. Joaquim had done a shoddy job of tying her up, and with a few tugs the rope gave a bit. Dolores pulled as if her life depended on it, which it did. By the time she managed to free herself, there was a ring of blood around her shins and ankles. She checked the front and back doors, and they were both locked, as she had feared. The new glass door in the kitchen gallery was impact-resistant, something the glazier had mentioned when he installed it.

Dolores was undeterred. She stumbled to the telephone. Jacint was alarmed by Dolores's raspy, stuttering voice; he anxiously asked her what was wrong, and she blurted out words without realizing that nothing she said made much sense.

'They killed my father back in Colorado Moon so I had to flee,' she rambled to Jacint. 'A disgusting old man helped me because he was friends with my father or something and I came here because that old man was a friend of Quim's, and Quim wanted to raise me, so he adopted me, but now he tortures me, he has tied me up and locked me inside the flat, and he killed my dog Vulgar who I loved so much. He is raving mad and now I am locked up. I need help. I have to get away soon, so he won't find me and do to me what he—'

Jacint asked Dolores to slow down, he tried to calm and reassure her, though hearing her utter such nonsense was scary, it set his pulse racing. But what followed was more inarticulate ranting. A bewildered Jacint fell silent, not knowing what to do and at the same time realising that something must be done and he was the one called upon to do it, for as a doctor he had been trained to help others. It broke Jacint's heart to see such a beautiful and unique girl delirious. He couldn't think straight. He promised Dolores he would be right over, ignoring her comment about her not being able to open the door to let him in. Why wouldn't she be able to open the door? He wondered whether Dolores had taken a fall, perhaps off a ladder, and whether shock was preventing her from speaking and reasoning properly. He rushed out and headed to Joaquim's place.

When Joaquim returned to the flat, Jacint was ringing the doorbell and pounding on the front door. As he made his way up the stairs, he heard some of the conversation between Jacint and Dolores.

'I can't open up! I can't!'

'Dolores, just turn the key in the lock.'

'I can't!'

'Please, Dolores!'

'Go away, Jacint, leave now. Or he'll come back and trap you too.'

Joaquim climbed the rest of the stairs calmly and put his arm around Jacint's shoulders.

'I'm so glad you came, Jacint,' he said with a sadness that was not altogether feigned. 'I'm terribly concerned about Dolores; she seems to be having some kind of mental breakdown. Let me open the door. I had to lock it when I went out. I couldn't locate a doctor over the phone, and the emergency services refused to send a psychiatrist over. I didn't know what to do. I locked the doors to prevent Dolores from doing something terrible. If you could help me, Jacint, if you could only help us. Ah, Jacint, I would be so very grateful ... '

He unlocked the door as he said this, and then Dolores threw her arms around the young man's neck. A despondent-looking Joaquim bent down and whispered to Jacint: 'See if you can calm her down, and if you do, come and talk to me. We must help this poor girl.'

29
THE SECOND STEP (DESCENDING): GAVEL (B)

QUIM AND JACINT WERE IN THE STUDY, AND DOLORES WAS asleep. Jacint had noticed that Dolores had been given a shot, and he had faint misgivings about it, but Joaquim mentioned the tranquilliser. Maybe he should have waited for a doctor, he said, but he couldn't find one, and when Dolores became hysterical, he panicked. He volunteered the dose and type of sedative he'd used, and the young man nodded and asked what had happened.

Joaquim's account, even if improvised, had the tenor of truth, no one would have doubted him. An attack of hysterics or something of the sort. A knife pointed at him, then at herself. 'I had to restrain her,' he said in a trembling voice, and he appeared to be holding back tears. It had started with Dolores screaming at him that he had killed her dog, when in fact Vulgar had run away and had probably been hit by a car, the poor thing. 'You can't imagine the scene,' Joaquim said. 'Terrifying. I am still quite shaken.'

Jacint promised to find a good doctor, so they could determine what was wrong with Dolores and start treating her as soon as possible. Yes, yes, Joaquim said, but he would not allow them to section her, not under any circumstances. There was a silence. The sinister, the terrible, the painful image of madness flashed through Jacint's mind. He was instinctively assailed by the question: was the malady hereditary? We are all so mean spirited. The memory of half-forgotten textbooks surfaced like the remains of a shipwreck, a piece of driftwood popping up, then sinking, a bottle rising to the surface only to be sucked underwater again.

'It's late. Perhaps tomorrow—'

Tomorrow meant hope. A new dawn. The possibility of renewal.

'Should I stay the night?' Jacint offered. 'Maybe the two of us should keep watch over her.'

'No need for that,' Joaquim said, 'but do give me your number if you don't mind. I'm not sure I have it. I'll call you if anything happens.'

Joaquim didn't phone that night or the following day. It was Jacint who got in touch, and he was duly reassured. They had a doctor, and apparently it was going to be a long treatment. 'An episode of paranoia, most likely transient, and treatable,' Joaquim said. 'I've made it clear that under no circumstances will I have her put away, not unless it becomes absolutely necessary.'

Jacint didn't know there was no doctor, no diagnosis, no truth to Joaquim's words. He suspected nothing. He didn't know that the door to Joaquim's flat was always locked and bolted, that even the telephone was padlocked so only Joaquim could place and receive calls. And that Dolores wasn't ill, at least no more so than anyone is, but that she was a prisoner.

He phoned a couple of times a day, and Joaquim always told him that things were slowly improving but it would be better for him to stay away for the time being, it was for the best; having people around upset Dolores. A week later, Jacint called only every other day, and after fifteen days his phone calls ceased. Dolores's spark had been extinguished. Sometimes Jacint felt a twinge of remorse, and then he told himself that he had not taken any serious steps in the relationship. A pretty girl, to be sure, and things could have been great, but then again ... no, better to just let it be. She didn't mean much to him. Too bad. She was so pretty!

Jon Carnisser died, sooner than even he could have predicted. Joaquim attended the funeral and sent a large flower wreath, while Dolores, who was locked up at home, languished under the effects of the strong sedative coursing through her veins. One day Ramon showed up at the flat unannounced. Joaquim sent him away, saying they were painting the walls and Dolores was downtown choosing new curtains. If anyone phoned or knocked on their door asking about Dolores, Joaquim told them she was visiting relatives in the States, and he wasn't sure when she'd be back. Every time someone showed up, Dolores had to be bound and gagged, and if she resisted, she was drugged.

The moment came when Dolores stopped fighting back and began to consider her situation. She could not communicate with anyone, but perhaps if she was clever enough ... She had to keep calm and go along with whatever Joaquim had in mind. And plot her escape. She had ample time to ponder things. Her change couldn't be too sudden. Joaquim knew her well; he was a cunning bastard. On the other hand, her planning could not be too drawn-out because he was capable of killing her. Would he do it? A physical confrontation was out of the question; he was much stronger than she was and would easily overpower her. Whatever it was, it had to be at night, when he was sleeping. Surely, he still slept. If only they could reach some kind of truce, and he would let down his guard. Oh, if only she could get her hands on that key! Her move had to be subtle; it had to be clever. Above all, she must be able to carry it out alone. It was plain now: she could count on no one. But could she stand on her own two feet?

Are you strong enough, Dolores?

After a great deal of thought, she had a plan.

'Don't tie me up, Quim. There's no need for that.' Her look of resignation was convincing. 'I promise I won't budge. I won't scream. I won't do anything at all. You can trust me.'

Joaquim left the rope on the chair, kissed Dolores on the forehead and went to answer the door; some large parcels were being delivered, and he had to sign for them. The man who handed him the delivery slip was only there for a moment, but Joaquim's heart was pounding as he glanced over his shoulder and strained to listen for any sounds. She didn't do anything. Just as promised. When he had put the boxes away in his study, Joaquim went back to Dolores's room.

She was sitting calmly on the bed.

'See?'

'So, you've decided to change your tune?'

'Not exactly, but it won't do me any good to scream my head off or cry for help.'

'What kind of talk is this? As if you were in any danger, Dolores. How could you possibly believe I could hurt you?'

The question was absurd under the circumstances, and Dolores was raging inside, but she didn't show it.

'Maybe we should talk, Quim.'

'Go ahead. I'm listening.'

'We can't go on like this.'

'And what am I supposed to do? You want to leave, and I don't want you to go. I have no other choice.'

'What if I promised to stay?'

'Oh, Dolores! I can't trust you any more. You've always deceived me. Always.'

'Just now, I said I wouldn't shout and I didn't. Right? Try me as many times as you want, Quim. You can't imagine how horrible it is to live like this. I'm a prisoner.'

'All right,' Joaquim said quite suddenly and with resolve. 'Get ready and we'll go out for a walk, you and me.'

Dolores drank in the fresh air, stared into the sun as her vision flickered, admired the shop windows, caressed a tree. Everything was so beautiful!

'I'm hurting too, Dolores,' Joaquim held her by the elbow without exerting any pressure as the two of them ambled along. 'It pains me deeply to see you looking so pale and not getting any sunlight. If you only knew … '

Dolores was on her best behaviour, she kept Joaquim happy, and his disposition slowly changed, though he continued to watch her closely. It wasn't so much that he didn't trust her but that he trusted no one.

One night after dinner Dolores suggested a game of chess. It was fun. Joaquim was beaming, he even let her win. They could be so happy together! He reached out his hand and placed it on Dolores's thin, white fingers. The subtlety and restraint of her acting was powerless against her instinctive reaction. She yanked her hand away as if burned by his touch. Joquim slunk off to bed feeling dejected.

I, too, once spat on the bald head of fools and raged at the sexless air of our sacristies. I was once haughty. Now I am a dog, and I beg to be allowed to cling to your side even if it's just for a moment.

A few days later, Dolores had a copy of one of the keys and the money from her bank account, the cash she had stashed away and a small suitcase holding a few essentials; she had her diamond ring in a safe place. It had required all her ingenuity, patience and cunning. She felt satisfied. This time, she would beat him.

This time, you fucking bastard, your luck has run out.

30
THE FIRST STEP (DESCENDING): RULER (A)

JOAQUIM WAS ASLEEP. DOLORES PUT HER EAR TO HIS BEDROOM door and heard him snoring. He was a light sleeper, so she had to be careful. If only she had managed to get her hands on some of those drops that have no taste but knock you out, and she could have slipped them into his food. If only she had dared to tie him up. Impossible. He would have woken up before the job was done. Dolores was frightened, her whole body shook, and she made more noise than she would have liked; her hands were like a caged bird's wings caressing the air from behind bars. She tripped over a chair and froze in terror. The snoring stopped. The living room tiles were cold against Dolores's bare feet. The snoring resumed. Dolores took a deep breath and tried to talk to herself.

You have nothing to lose any more, keep going, Dolores. So what if you get caught out? What else can this madman possibly do to you?

She dressed in the dark without making a sound, her heart beating like an air compressor. She tried to steady her nerves. Getting on her shoes was a struggle, as was putting her arm through the sleeve of her blouse, and where on earth were the buttonholes? Now the zip wouldn't budge, and that shoe belonged on her left foot, no? How she wished she could stop shaking!

She had a bag full of clothes, her savings sewn into the cuffs of her trousers, the ring on her finger—looking at it gave her such confidence! She had only been able to locate her old passport, issued to Dolores Mendoza. Had they ever applied for one in the name of Dolores Simon? It didn't matter. It would have to do, as it certainly had when she fled all those years ago. She had done well for herself in the intervening years. She would make her way to the airport, though not by taxicab, that would cost too much money, and every penny counted now. The night bus to Sants Railway Station then, and the airport shuttle from there. Certain recollections came to her as if slowly surfacing from the place deep within us all where our memories dwell.

No one would tell me how to get here; it took me ... it must've taken me four hours to find this street. I walked and walked. I was worn out with fatigue, and so hungry. Oh! Maybe I should take some food with me. But there's no need for that. Besides, I might make too much noise preparing it.

Now for the hardest part: opening the door, then closing it behind her. She could always leave it standing open. No, no. It might bang shut and wake him. Or perhaps ... She stood at the door and pulled it open one millimetre at a time, as slowly as if it weighed a thousand tonnes. The sound of Joaquim's snoring couldn't reach her there, but if he had heard anything he'd already be at the door, and then he would beat her and tie her up again. What else could he do to her?

It's almost over, Dolores. Hang on, Dolores. That is the street down there, and it leads to every other place in this big wide world.

Ah, to go home! She didn't really have a place she could call home, but she had to get back to where she came from, even if no one there would recognize her now. Maybe, if instead of that, she went ... Her thoughts were muddled, she had no wish to pursue the ideas in her mind. Her yearning to leave was so intense that it was her only goal. The door was cracked just enough to let her body and her travel bag through. And ... done! She was outside the apartment. Now, to close the door behind her, then lock it with the key. Getting a copy made had not been easy, but lately Joaquim had trusted her enough to let her go to the hair salon on her own. She knew he was following her, but he didn't think to trail the hairdresser, who was kind enough to take the key to the locksmith and have a copy made. Talk about a favour!

Dolores put the key in the lock to keep the door from making a noise when she closed it. Then she slowly shut the door and turned the key. Despite her precautions, the noise it made was not faint. The terror made the blood rush to her cheeks, the veins in her neck bulged as if trying to break free, just as she, too, wanted to break free. For a moment she stood frozen with fear, like a block of ice, a tree, a rock. Nothing happened. The stairs. The street door that opened inward. Then the street itself. The glowing lampposts. A chirping cricket that rubbed its wings together. The blueish tinge of the pavement, and a full moon garlanded by languid clouds.

Her footsteps resounded as if the asphalt were hollow, an eggshell, a watermelon rind. Clack-clack. Clack-clack. She slowly tiptoed away. The sloping street, down, down. What if she turned around? What if she turned around and saw him laughing on the balcony? What if she turned and he was trailing her, a weapon in hand, a rope, a syringe? It took real courage, but Dolores looked back. The street was deserted. The apartment building was a silhouette that was vanishing from view, like an ill-fated ship foundering at sea.

Dolores decided against the first bus stop, on Travessera de Gràcia. Too close to home, and sometimes the night bus took a long time to come. She walked on and ruled out the next stop, too. She waited at the third stop, beneath the shelter. Not a soul in sight. Every passing minute, every second, was pure agony. She kept casting nervous glances up the street but didn't see anyone. Then, for a brief moment, the world spun out of sight. A man was running towards her. But at the next corner he turned and disappeared. The bus arrived. Dolores got on and bought her ticket, unable to speak, her mouth completely dry. Her whole body ached. She felt like she had a fever.

The bus left her near Sants Railway Station. She was nearing salvation, but she couldn't breathe easy yet; she only exhaled when the airport shuttle pulled out of the station. She got off at the entrance to the international terminal. There were more people in the departure hall than she had anticipated. Maybe there was a strike, or flights were delayed. If she could remember how to pray, she would.

Please, God. Please, God. Let there be a plane for me!

It was five-thirty in the morning; there was a six o'clock flight to New York, but there were no seats left.

'Should I put you on standby?' said the lady at the check-in counter. 'There's always someone who doesn't show up at the last minute. Statistics prove it! It's always the case, no matter where in the world.'

'Is there no other flight?' Dolores asked.

There was not. Dolores would have to wait until tomorrow or the following day. She had no choice but to allow that smiling woman in uniform to put her name on the standby list.

She made her way to the cafeteria and collapsed on a chair, spent but relatively calm. If she managed to get a seat on that plane, she would be out of Joaquim's reach. She would have something to drink and then hover by the check-in desk to make sure she got a ticket, should one become available. For now, she couldn't move, she was too exhausted. No one was waiting on the tables, so Dolores got up and went to the serving counter. She ordered a *cafè amb llet*. Anything to eat with that? No, she wouldn't be able to swallow a bite. After having her coffee, she'd go to the bathroom and put on some make-up. She was probably looking very pale, as if she had bleached her skin.

A sip of coffee, how good it was, how comforting! Then a hand grabbed her arm. She knew it was Joaquim before she turned to look. He was wearing his coat over his pyjamas. He looked dishevelled. Dolores noticed he didn't have any socks on. She couldn't remember if she had already paid, but if she had not maybe a waiter would come over and say, listen, Senyoreta ...

Then she was in Joaquim's car, sobbing loudly as they flew through Barcelona on the way back to the flat.

Dolores didn't know what was in the syringe, but it didn't have the same effect as other times. She felt relaxed but not sleepy, and there was a tingling sensation at the base of her neck, as if she was laughing. She didn't know what was happening, but she was calm, not at all anxious. A sense of wellbeing spread through her body.

Now she found herself in a straight-backed chair with armrests, her head thrust back against the headrest. How strange, Quim was placing a garland of flowers on her forehead. But why was he opening her mouth? She started to laugh but found she could not, and she wondered what could be so funny and why she was unable to laugh. Both her forehead and chin were strapped back, the tightness forcing her mouth open. Daylight flooded the room. Joaquim was opening a bunch of boxes and removing things from them.

'I'll put it to you straight,' he told her. 'Stay still. Do not move. If you do, this will hurt a lot. Understood? I've never hurt you before, so I trust I can count on you to cooperate. Look, Dolores, I've got to do this, okay? It's necessary. Absolutely necessary. It's for your own good, you see, this will stop you from seeing other people or giving yourself to another man. I must make you repulsive, Dolores. It's the only way. I am sorry, believe me I am. Sorrier than even you will be.'

Dolores couldn't speak, but she still had some of her mental faculties, and she roused herself from her torpor. 'What are you doing, Quim? Why? Don't hurt me. Don't hurt me!' But the only sounds that came out of her mouth were moans.

Joaquim narrated the procedure as he went. Dolores writhed in vain. Immobilised. Stupefied. Undone.

'Getting hold of this equipment was no easy feat,' Joaquim said. 'That idiot at the dental supply office kept insisting on seeing my professional credentials. He was a real bore! It took brains to justify my need for these outdated tools. I couldn't for the life of me procure an air turbine device! Too cumbersome. And besides, I worked with a dentist for a while, and I only know how to operate this kind of electric device.'

There was no need to be scared; it didn't have to hurt. He told her to stay still: despite her being tied up, he could accidentally pierce the roof of her mouth.

'That would be terrible,' he said, 'and I wouldn't know what to do. How would I explain it to a doctor? Okay. Now, I'm going to inject your gums with a strong dose of novocaine. Two shots and we're done; you won't even feel the second one, your gums will be like wood. It'll be just like going to the dentist. I'm doing this for you, Dolores, to protect you from yourself. Once the painkiller wears off it might hurt a bit, but don't worry, we've got plenty of drugs. Ah, my darling, I am so very sorry!'

The hand piece was fitted with a drill that was about two centimetres long and one millimetre wide. The drill bit was made of diamond.

'I have to warn you,' Joaquim said. 'You won't look pretty, no one will ever kiss you again, it would be unthinkable. But to me you'll be the same. We don't need anybody else, you and me.'

That horrifying sound began. The drill found its way to the tips of her upper teeth and slowly carved them into four terrifying triangles like shark teeth. Dolores gave guttural screams even though she felt no pain. She choked on her own saliva and Joaquim had to stop to allow her to breathe. He put a glass of water to her lips so she could have a sip, but the water dripped from her mouth and soaked her blouse.

It took for ever.

Dolores fainted. When she came to, she was in her own bed, a terrible pain in her mouth. She looked in the mirror and let out a bloodcurdling scream. The flat was closed up and Joaquim was gone. Dolores tore through the place breaking everything in sight as she searched for some kind of pain relief. Her lips were swollen. Her blood-streaked tongue looked like the skin of a lizard. She was like a wild animal that had just bitten into the still-throbbing flesh of a dying victim.

It was a terrifying sight. A girl howling in pain, her teeth four jagged fangs, her lips bloodied, sores in her mouth. Screaming in agony, completely mad.

PART FOUR
WHITE

CHAPTER XI – HIRAM

31
THE FIRST STEP (DESCENDING): RULER (B)

Eyes weeping, face filled with terror
hair yanked with great howls.

THE LINES IN THE MEDIEVAL POEM APTLY DESCRIBED HER state as she ran down the street, having opened the door with her own copy of the key, the one she had so ingeniously obtained, and which was still hidden in her bag. Joaquim, his thoughts elsewhere, his mind as lacerated as Dolores's lips and teeth, had not thought to look there.

The journey starts with open arms,
with wet eyes.

Dolores had become a wild, howling beast, the unwitting image of a fallen Cinderella. Half-mad with pain, her lips swollen, her blouse soaked with blood, one foot bare (where had she lost a shoe?), whimpering and dishevelled, she desperately sought relief, any form of relief, from the harrowing agony, the burning torment, the hammering pain in her mouth. A few passersby stopped and stared, and one charitable soul came forward to try to help this girl in distress, who trembled all over as she ran. But no one dared get too close, for it was plain that she was deranged. Who but a madwoman would show herself in public in such a state?

Finally, on an unfamiliar street, Dolores came across a plaque on a door announcing a dental office. She could not make out the name, but she thought that orthodontist meant dentist. How ignorant could she be, or did she not remember that orthodontist, like ophthalmologist, came from the Greek? Had she learnt so little from all the painstaking lessons she had received? So she climbed the stairs and pressed hard on the bell without lifting her finger. Open up! Open up! An indignant nurse answered the door, ready to call the police on the ill-mannered brute who was ringing the doorbell like that. But the sight of someone in dire need of help immediately silenced her. This was someone truly desperate. She alerted the doctor, who immediately let Dolores in and showed her to a room that was set up to treat dental emergencies. He gave Dolores an injection for the raging pain in her mouth and went to apologize to the fat patient in the main examination room. The woman sighed with relief at the unexpected reprieve. She said her problem could wait; one should react to such situations with compassion and mercy, as would Allah Himself. 'Go right ahead, doctor,' she said. 'No problem at all.'

The dentist was a boyish-looking man of about forty, with blond hair, metal-rimmed glasses, and a rather smarmy disposition. He had soft lips and child-like features, but his hands were strong and skilled. After administering a painkiller, he examined Dolores. In vain he asked her, as she sat there with her mouth open, offering no resistance, exhausted from pain and despair and her mad race through the streets, *who* had done such a vicious thing to her. It was certainly not the work of a dentist or any other kind of qualified professional, he told her in the one-sided conversation. Instead, it would meet the legal definition of torture. She should report it to the police. There could be no possible justification for such a heinous act, not to mention the personal violation it had entailed. The usual authorities and all their known affiliates, from police to lawyers, judges to gaolers, should be notified without delay. Dolores thought that Joaquim would have just laughed at this and said, Oh right—the Law! Which sanctioned theft on a grand scale and abuse by the rich and powerful, and had been created, there was that too, just to keep people from killing each another, horrid beasts that we are, all of us without exception and from the day we are born. As he tended to the girl, the doctor grew increasingly enraged thinking about how complicated it was to deal with the authorities, and about all the inevitable hurdles they forced people through.

The whole thing took a long time; at one point the nurse came in and asked the doctor what to tell the people in the waiting room who were wondering what the matter was and complaining that they didn't have all day, they had other things to do. One's wait is always long and tries one's patience. The patients would have to be rescheduled; the dentist said he would need a couple of hours to finish the job. Despite the weak jawline and soft lips, despite his childlike grin, he is at heart a hero, and promised to work overtime the following day, he would need to do that to be at peace with himself, and even with the Law, if it came to that.

He performed what was called an endodontic procedure. Dolores allowed him to treat her, dismissing her anguish for now, there would be enough time to face it later. Her tears were dry, only a trace of them was left, a little snail trail down her cheeks as a reminder of the pain she had endured. 'Who could've done such a thing?' the perplexed dentist said every now and then. And surprisingly, this short, bewildered question of his comforted Dolores more than any serious talk could have done. 'He was no dentist, that's for sure. What evil beast, what kind of sadist or madman?'

The nurse told everyone in the waiting room that they would need to reschedule their appointments because the doctor was performing an emergency procedure on the distressed girl who had just come in. It was an emergency. Surely, they could understand. Some of the patients grumbled; those who had witnessed Dolores's arrival said it was fine; they would wait or return the following day.

The doctor fitted provisional crowns over Dolores's teeth. She would need to have more permanent dental work done, but at least she wouldn't be in pain any more, and she wouldn't cut her tongue and lips. He gave her a red, strawberry-flavoured gel. 'It'll cure your sores,' he said. He wrote her a prescription and told her to take a certain painkiller as needed. 'I'll make you an appointment to have your teeth fixed properly.' He encouraged her to go to the police and said that she could count on him to provide a written description of her initial state, but his words stemmed more from compassion than conviction, and he didn't have the heart to grill Dolores about her ordeal, because she was weeping again and looked so feeble. He was a decent man, this dentist, he did his best for her, but suddenly he seemed to grow a bit wary and suspicious. He and the nurse talked while Dolores tried to gather herself. 'The ghastly things one comes across in this profession!'

Dolores assured them she would file a police report, for she had been kidnapped by a lunatic. Voicing this among normal people felt so strange! She was so grateful for the dental work and wanted to pay extra. She would be back. Tomorrow, she said, but then she contradicted herself by telling them that she was going away on a trip. She tried to explain what had happened to her, but her account was mostly incoherent; she talked about running away and about her fear of being caught, and again promised to file a police report, she most definitely would, yes, but now she had a plane to catch.

'I hope you'll understand that I can't work for free,' the dentist said. Dolores's bad lip made speaking difficult, and it took her a long time to make herself understood. But finally, she got what she wanted, which was to leave. They accepted the ring she took off her finger as payment and let her go. 'I assure you it's a good diamond,' Dolores told them. They gave her a white lab coat that was in a cupboard to wear over her stained blouse. And seeing that Dolores was missing a shoe and that her own street shoes were in the coat closet, the nurse let her have her white clogs.

Dolores made her way to the airport, her money still sewn into the cuffs of her trousers. This time she was lucky: her flight was in a few minutes and there was a seat for her on the plane. It was an expensive ticket, costing nearly all her cash.

The lab coat she had on was too large, and the nurse's slip-ons too small. Dolores looked like a gypsy in disguise, dishevelled, her lips red and swollen. She was leaving as she had arrived: a sorry sight. She reapplied the soothing gum gel. Victòria's pendant hung from her neck, the one thing she had wanted to take with her. Stripped of material possessions then as now, Dolores had rebounded from one side of the Atlantic to the other, like a ball bouncing off a wall.

Seated on the plane, she told herself that she was really Dorothy Gardner using a fake passport, that she belonged in Colorado Moon and thought and spoke in English. Her identity had been slowly eroded, but its core was mostly intact, locked away at the back of her brain, just as she herself had been imprisoned in body and mind for all those years.

Now, she was free.

The workings of memory quicken certain recollections. She knew where she was headed and what she wanted, she knew what she knew. And yet, at the same time, she knew nothing at all. She pictured Joaquim's face and felt a deep, inexplicable sorrow.

Oh, Quim! We could have been so happy together!
Oh, Quim! What will I do without you now?

She didn't know how she would manage without him or if she would know how to live her life. She didn't know if one day she would be able to fill the deep void in her soul left by the man who, besotted, had kept vigil as she slept.

You loved me so much!
You love me so much, Joaquim!

The plane took off.

32

JOAQUIM RETURNED TO THE FLAT LOADED WITH PAINKILLERS, devastated by his own savagery and pursued to the edge of reason by the memory of Dolores's screams. But at the sight of the front door standing open, he was overcome with rage and terror.

Dolores was gone.

To the airport!

He was already running. He had to catch her. He had to make it.

He must get her back!

Dolores was entering the international terminal. She looked scruffy and dirty, like a gypsy. He was about to run after her, and then ... and then something made him stop. In a sudden flash of recognition, he understood that he was nothing but a classic fool, a silly old man. A harsh look at himself made him come to his senses. He stood frozen in place, as if pinned to the ground, like a butterfly trapped inside a cardboard box. And then a wave of tenderness, of true love, enveloped him as he watched her go. He adored Dolores with every thread of his being, his very soul, with all the devotion a human being is capable of. As no one had ever loved before.

You're leaving.

You're leaving, and the trees shed their leaves as you go, the blood of hundreds of birds that nested there trickles down the bark. Time stops, though only for me. I will bathe twice, a thousand times over, in the same place in the river.

He leaned against the window that gave onto the tarmac. The plane, like a timid worm, slithered down the runway.

What had happened to him, and when did he lose his mind? Was it when she arrived? When suddenly he grew terrified at the thought of growing old? When did he realize that she would never love him back?

To think that he had never touched her, while that swine Jack had had her for himself!

To think that he could be driven to madness over his love for a girl!

He could track her down in America. He could find her, sure. But he had been vanquished, and he must now have the dignity to concede defeat. The bitterness was impossible to deny. She had beaten him at his own game and tossed him aside like a lipstick-stained napkin after a scrumptious meal, useless, dirty, and wrinkled.

How would he live without her?

His rancour felt like the millstone around the neck of a suicide.

So, what am I now? What is this place, this moment? Undone, I rage against my downfall. It would be easy to conclude that I came into this world with a dagger under my arm. But even in defeat I remain standing amid the nothingness that follows war. I have not retreated. And I do not wish to die. How else would I savour the fact that you have abandoned me?

His old maxims rescued him from despair: if destiny brings you shame, blame your pride, for it is in the fulfilment of your destiny, rather than in destiny itself, where all honour lies, and shame as well.

Gazing at the aeroplane as it roared and gathered speed, he thought:

Oh, Dolores!
We could have been happy, so very happy,
I had so much love for you!

Dazzled from looking at the sky and at that little worm that was taking off with the pride of a golden eagle, Quim smiled with satisfaction at having loved so deeply.

It was a rare privilege.

33

AS THE AEROPLANE TOOK OFF, MUSIC PLAYED IN DOLORES'S EAR.
Tod und Verzweiflung flammet um mich her!
How Quim loved *The Magic Flute*!
So bist du meine Tochter nimmermehr.
Verstossen sei auf ewig, verlassen sei auf ewig,
Zertrümmert sei'n auf ewig alle Bande der Natur.

What would she do without him?

The plane soared into the air, retracting the wheels under its belly. It looked like an arrow, a giant finger pointed at the sky, cleaving the clouds as it rose.

What a heavy price she had paid!

Then, almost inaudibly, Dolores murmured to herself:

'Come on, Dorothy—let's go hunt some rats!'

On the ground below, a turtle-faced Quim watched the plane with his mouth half open, spellbound, strangely serene.

The aircraft, unwavering like the needle in Dolores's embroidered cushion, traversed a mass of clouds, rising further, drawing a pattern that would never be finished.

ISABEL-CLARA SIMÓ (ALCOI, 1943 – BARCELONA, 2020) WAS a renowned Valencian author. She was born in Alcoi and became well-known for creating complex characters involved in complicated relationships, as can be seen in her famous works, such as *Júlia, Històries perverses*, and *La Salvatge (The Wild One)*. Simó's literary journey led to her being highly praised, including winning the Sant Jordi Prize for *La salvatge (The Wild One)* and the Creu de Sant Jordi for her contributions to literature. During her career, Simó worked in journalism and literature, showing that she was talented in many areas. Isabel-Clara Simó has had a big impact on modern Valencian and Catalan literature and is a well-known figure in the world of books.

MARTHA TENNENT AND MARUXA RELAÑO ARE A MOTHER-DAUGHTER translation team. They have translated a number of works from Spanish and Catalan, including *I'll Do Anything You Want*, by Iolanda Batallé, *Dead Lands*, by Núria Bendicho, *War, So Much War* and *Garden by the Sea*, by Mercè Rodoreda, *Blood Crime*, by Sebastià Alzamora, and *The Sea*, by Blai Bonet. They are both recipients of National Endowment for the Arts fellowships for their translation work. Martha was previously dean of the School of Translation at the University of Vic, Barcelona. Maruxa worked as a journalist in New York and was a translation editor for the *Wall Street Journal*. They live in Barcelona.

ESPERANZA MANZANERA FERRÁNDIZ (VELMOCK) WAS BORN IN Valencia, Spain, into a household where her father was a painter and her mother was a literature enthusiast. She has lived in Granada since 2017, where she is a secondary school philosophy teacher. After making several forays into the literary and cinematic worlds, she discovered her true vocation in the art world, mainly dedicating herself to photography and its post-production using various digital techniques, such as photo painting, collage and photomontage. Her main influences stem from the fantastic art of René Magritte, Giorgio de Chirico, Georgia O'Keeffe, Remedios Varo and James Ensor. Expressionism and surrealism are arguably the artistic movements most closely associated with her work. She has the honour of having some very exciting awards, mentions and publications on her CV, including Life Framer, I Premio de Lo Raro, Bizarro y Bello, Beautiful Bizarre Magazine and Cultura Inquieta, as well as individual and collective exhibitions, one of which is permanent in Boadilla de Rioseco (Palencia), where 'Lágrimas de Esperanza' is exhibited alongside works by Antonio López, Luis Gordillo and many other artists.

Since 2020, she has been a member of MAV (Mujeres en las Artes Visuales).

We translate female authors who write in minority languages. Only women. Only minority languages. This is our choice.

We know that we only win if we all win, that's why we are proud to be fair trade publishers. And we are committed to supporting organisations that help women to live freely and with dignity.

We are 3TimesRebel.